CW00520231

A SENSE OF TRUTH

By Paul Knight

"And now each night, and all night long,

Over those plains still roams the Dong;

And above the wail of the Chimp and Snipe

You may hear the squeak of his plaintive pipe

While he seeks, but seeks in vain

To meet with his Jumbly Girl again."

Edward Lear

CHAPTER 1

JUNE 2015

"Great Lord guide us. Great Lord guide us. Great Lord guide us," she said.

He ignored her. She had hardly stopped all morning. He was focused on the task in hand. Everything was working exactly as it should. The Great Lord's plans could not be interrupted. The forecast had threatened rain, but the Great Lord had provided a clear sky. This was no surprise, of course. Prayer had guided them to the right path and the Great Lord's will had never been clearer.

The van seemed to be moving too slowly, but he had set the rules this way. No speeding, no sort of driving that could attract any attention. It was a big ask for the young man behind the wheel, and although the preparations had been thorough, driving on the opposite side of the road to what he was used to required intense concentration.

They were passing through the edge of the town now. There was risk here. People. Sinners. They were so close to their prayers finally being answered. His senses seemed to heighten, and he noticed every detail around him. The people here knew nothing of the truth of the world. Look at them; not one of them appeared capable of serious thought. The women's shorts were too short and their tops too tight. And were those two men holding hands? He felt a sadness that he knew their destiny and they did not. Part of him wanted to stop the van and show them. He could correct them. If they only knew the truth. But it was everywhere, and this was not his mission. And in any case, they disgusted him.

"Are those the woods?" she asked.

They were, and the intensity level inside the van rose again.

"Is she there . . . are they there?" she added, but he was still ignoring her.

This was a practical task suited to a man's temperament. He had not really wanted her to come at all, but she had convinced him she may be needed. It was possible a woman's touch could be useful. And it would perhaps have been a little cruel to leave her behind.

He called the van in front, checked locations and timings, nodded once or twice and then hung up, content.

"The Great Lord is bringing them to us exactly as anticipated," he said. For the first time since they started out that morning, he looked her straight in the eye. "The time is here. Be strong, the Great Lord will guide us." He put his hand on hers, squeezed it, and looked away again.

His heart was racing as they pulled into the car park. True joy overcame him as he scanned the area and saw that it was empty. A laugh burst out of him. What a fool he had been to ever doubt it. They had been prepared to simply drive off and keep repeating the plan until the area was clear. The element of chance had helped him to stay calm, knowing that nothing might happen today, but now, with the realisation that this really was the time, he felt lightheaded. His breath was short, and his legs felt heavy. *Stick to the plan*, he thought.

A young woman emerged from a path through the woods into the car park, her toddler beside her, swishing a stick around in the air.

Three young men jumped out from the vans. They had practised the grab. Two of them went for the woman. One wrapped his arm fully around her from behind, and the other clamped his hand over her mouth. The third man scooped up the child, covering his mouth too.

They bundled the woman into the back of the first van, one man with her. The doors slammed shut. The other man took the child into the back of the second van.

"Let's start," the older man said, and he and the woman left the cab to join the child in the back. He noticed that he could hear no sound from the other van and was pleased that their preparations were paying off. The vans left in convoy.

•

"Stop fighting, you need to listen to what happens next."

The back of the van that held the mother had been padded out for soundproofing and fitted with a bench to sit on, but it was otherwise empty. They had anticipated a fight, but the young man had underestimated the wild destruction of a mother defending her child. He was bleeding from across the cheek, his top lip and his left hand, where bite marks were visible. He had clear instructions not to hurt her and worried that he may have failed with this, but what else could he do? He had to hold her tight to get any sense of control.

She stopped struggling when her child's voice came through the speakers.

"Mummy," the child said, but was cut off as he started to ask a question.

"We have him in the van in front," said the man, "and if you can't convince me that you will settle down, they will go one way and we will go another." To make sure he was being absolutely clear, he added, "and you will never see him again."

She pushed herself into the side of the van and pulled her knees up to her chest. Looking him hard in the eye, she knew.

"It's you, isn't it?"

CHAPTER 2

Saric was in the client office of his house, focused on the computer screen in front of him. When they had first met, Rob had wondered if Saric was spending too much time with his computer and not enough on the streets. Rob's view then of a private detective was informed only from books and films. In reality, as Saric had explained at the time, the role of a private detective is predominantly to accumulate facts. Facts break lies. Facts lead to connections. Facts solve cases.

Rob sat in his usual chair in the office, off to the side of the room. He listened with interest to the latest evolution of Saric's great success, Sense Check, which had originally been designed to cross-check information and confirm which version of events could be true. Its earlier incarnation was largely limited to checking dates, times and distances. Could the suspect really have got from London to Brighton by car in an hour and a half on a Saturday? Was there time for the suspect to meet someone on their journey from home to work that morning? Saric would manually populate Sense Check with key data from witness statements, any background information available online and his own observations. From this, the program would identify inconsistencies.

In the years since, Saric had refined and expanded Sense Check's capabilities. Online data gathering was now almost completely automatic, and, therefore, pretty much instant and vast in its range. More recently, advances in artificial intelligence had been another leap forward. Sense Check was now learning how to validate online data and assess website reliability, and Saric had plans to direct it to be able to recognise language patterns that indicated lying. But today was all about Saric's latest upgrade.

"Have you turned on the speech module?" Rob asked.

Saric looked up from the screen. "Yes, and it's working perfectly, thank you." He was sitting at his grand oak desk, which he claimed was made with wood recovered from a ship that fought at the Battle of Trafalgar. Rob was not sure if that was true, but he hoped so.

"Give it a try," said Saric, "test it."

"OK," said Rob, "it's on now, right?" Saric nodded. "What do you want me to test it with?"

Sense Check showed the content of their discussion along the bottom of the screen; the different elements of the conversation scrolled across it. So far, all the small talk was grey. More important content would move across the screen in varying colours. Statements worth testing should be yellow. Insufficiently supported claims were displayed in blue. Blatant lies should be red.

"Give it a logical conclusion," said Saric.

"I think, therefore I am," said Rob.

Conclusion incomplete, suggest further testing, recommended Sense Check.

"Very funny," said Saric. "Try a proper one."

"Oh, OK, then," said Rob. "Here goes . . . I bought a cake on Wednesday to give to my mum. I gave it to her on Tuesday."

Saric watched with some pride as Sense Check flagged a possible logical inconsistency and told him to validate the dates more accurately.

Rob was genuinely impressed at Saric's latest module. This was the first truly real-time development, and it opened up some intriguing possibilities.

"Have you done all the pull throughs yet?" Rob asked.

"All the ones I can think of for now. Check this out." Saric clicked his mouse a couple of times and started talking. "On the third of February, I was in Bath. I was wearing shorts and a t-shirt."

Sense Check tested the statement. It checked the weather in Bath that day, the local news for traffic alerts, unusual building closures, and so on. Anything that could invalidate the statement or provide Saric with a fact or two to test a possible lie with. Sense Check's message read, *Weather and clothing inconsistent*, and next to it provided supporting details about the temperature, the level of rainfall, and the time the sun had set on that day.

Saric went on to explain some of the testing he had been running, and the post real-time reporting Sense Check could provide after an interview had concluded. Rob's favourite test was when Saric set Sense Check the task of listening to thirty minutes of news on the morning radio. The normal procession of journalists, politicians and expert commentators came and went, with Sense Check listening to it all. In the resulting report, only four per cent of the entire content was not greyed out as irrelevant in nature. Of the four per cent it determined as worth flagging up, almost all of it was made up of conclusions that were either logically incoherent or could not be accepted without further testing, or both.

Saric wondered whether natural, day-to-day conversations would give rise to more relevant content than the stage-managed debates held on the radio.

The doorbell chimed. Saric took a look at their guest on his screen via the front door camera. He had taught himself to ignore all first impressions. All impressions generally.

CHAPTER 3

Rob got up to let their guest in. He always let the guest in the first time they arrived; he appreciated the opportunity to get a sense of someone before talking business.

"A handshake is not a fact," Saric would tell him.

"True," Rob would reply, "but crimes are committed by people, not computers."

The opening moments of a new case held a great deal of fascination for Rob. In general, he had always found people interesting, and particularly so at moments of tension. Why people behave the way they do is the great mystery of life. As he walked down the stairs, he contemplated how little he and Saric had been told so far. Saric only worked from referrals these days, and this one had come from an old contact who knew better than to try and tell him anything about the case herself. They just knew a middle-aged woman had been killed in a hotel room. She was suffocated in her bed. No signs of a break in.

Nothing stolen. And the statistics indicated Rob was about to open the door to her murderer.

"Good evening," he said.

"Hello, I'm Phillip. I have a meeting with Saric. Is this the right place?"

"Yes, this is it. He works from home. I'm Rob. I work with Saric." Rob offered his hand to shake and paid attention to the position of his guest's hand as he accepted the offer. There was a dominant aspect to it, encouraging Rob's hand to be slightly under his. As he took hold, Rob gently corrected it to exactly even. "Come in and I'll show you up," he said.

Phillip's suit was expensive, possibly tailored. He wore a white, cuff-linked shirt. His face was nearly handsome and partially covered in a well-groomed beard, with hints of white coming through. If he had been good looking in his youth, it had been slowly eroded through too much coffee, not enough sleep and an excess of self-importance. He looked like he had come straight from work, which annoyed Rob, given the circumstances.

Rob let Phillip pass him to go up the stairs first. He took the stairs fast and he had a wiry athleticism to him that made Rob think he might be a jogger, or worse, a cyclist. If the latter was true, it was unlikely Rob was going to like this man.

Rob opened the office door and allowed Phillip to enter. Saric was sat at his desk, still focused on his monitor. He did not look up.

"Take a seat," said Rob. Rob had been experimenting recently with different chair decision options. For this meeting, given their guest had just lost his wife in the most tragic way, Rob had chosen one of the gentler tests. Three chairs were lined up against the wall so that the guest would have to select one to move to the desk. They were all basic plastic chairs that looked like they should be in a school classroom. One was red, one yellow and one blue. At one level, it was interesting to hypothesise as to the extent that the true mood of the guest would be represented by their colour choice. For Saric, there were far too many variables to determine anything from anyone's choice; a point that Rob had largely accepted. He still liked to guess, though. At a more practical level, he liked to interrupt their psychological pattern. He had observed over the years that a visit to a private detective was such an unusual encounter for the average person that they had no true frame of reference for it and would often adopt a defensive mindset, as if being brought before the headmaster to be disciplined. As Saric had flat-out refused to conduct interviews from anywhere other than behind his desk, Rob had been playing around with other ways to alter the guest's mindset. By being forced to make the active selection of a chair, and move it to the position of their choice, he thought they may shake off some of the passive sense of being interviewed. Sadly, there was no real way of knowing whether it made any difference at all.

Rob sat off to the side of the room as Phillip picked up the red chair and placed it directly in front of Saric. He sat forward in the chair, tried crossing his legs and changed his mind. Saric finally looked up.

"So," he said, "what can we do for you?"

"I have a problem and I'm told you might be the man to help me out. Do you already know what's happened?"

"I understand your wife has been murdered," said Saric. "Please accept my condolences. I hope we can help you at what must be a very difficult time."

"Thank you and yes, this is a difficult time," said Phillip. "My wife was killed. I have no idea why. She was just an accountant. I just can't see why anyone would want to do this. The police say it was more like an execution. An execution! What the hell is that supposed to mean? Who executes a middle-aged accountant? They say there were no signs of a break in. I can't believe she was having an affair; I would have noticed something, wouldn't I? She just wasn't the type." He paused for a moment.

"The police are very successful at solving crimes of this type, Phillip. Before you go on, do you know what it is you would like of us?" said Saric.

"The police–" Phillip spat the word out "–do not seem interested in solving anything. Jane and I had not exactly been close for some time." He looked across at Rob and then back to Saric. "I have been seen with someone else. Motive, apparently. Ha! As if I would risk a life in prison for her. But the real problem is that I can't prove where I was that night. The bloody dog. The stupid bloody dog. I never wanted it in the first place. I was out with the bloody thing for hours and now I can't show them anything to prove where I was."

Phillip seemed to think this should be a sufficient explanation, but Saric did not react at all.

"The police," he tried again, "think it was me."

Saric sat upright in his chair, dipped his head a little and looked Phillip in the eye. It looked to Rob like Saric was about to suck the truth straight out of Phillip's face. Phillip held the gaze for a moment, and then looked away. For the first time, Rob noticed how tired Phillip seemed. He looked like a man who had been tired for a very long time.

"It wasn't me," Phillip said in answer to the question that was not asked. "I need you to prove it wasn't me. Can you do that?"

"To be clear, are you asking us to find a way to prove it was not you, or do you want us to investigate what actually happened? Generally, I would suggest that it is easier to prove something that is, rather than something that is not."

"Look, I need you to tell me what I need. If you tell me finding who did this is the way to go then fine, let's do that," said Phillip. "How much is this going to cost?" he added.

"I don't need your money," said Saric. "You will pay me back in time. For every hour I spend on your case, you pay me back with an hour of what you can do. I understand you are an architect. Maybe you can build me something. We'll figure it out."

"What if my time is more valuable than yours?"

"It's not," said Saric, before adding, "Right then, we better get started. What I would like you to do is tell us everything you know about the circumstances leading up to the attack. This may include some wider history. I appreciate this may be difficult for you, but you must be absolutely honest and full in your responses. Please try and keep the facts clean; if you are unsure as to whether a statement is true please say so. My associate and I will interrupt you as necessary. Please bear with us even when the questions seem irrelevant to you. We will not waste your time. Are you ready?"

Phillip sat back in his chair and let out a deep breath. He accepted the terms of the discussion.

Until now, Saric had largely ignored Sense Check's feed on his monitor. The text of the conversation had flowed across the screen largely in irrelevant grey. It had raised a question about why Phillip's 'bloody dog' was covered in blood, which Saric had dismissed, and he made a mental note to double check whether a UK-specific swearword speech recognition element was available yet. Now came Sense Check's first real test.

Over the next few minutes, Saric collected the basic details about Phillip (two 'l's) and his late wife, Jane. It was an unremarkable tale of a middle-aged couple. No children, allegedly through choice, which had allowed them to stay focused on work. Jane was a partner in a high street accountancy practice. She had one business partner, an older gentleman edging towards the end of his career. Phillip owned a small but highly successful architectural business. Sense Check pulled up the accounts for both businesses and confirmed levels of profitability, particularly from Phillip's business, sufficient to corroborate his account of their wealth. Phillip was having a somewhat feeble affair with one of his staff. He seemed to take so little joy from it that Rob wondered if his heart was really in it, or perhaps he just thought that was what people like him did. As far as Phillip knew, Jane was not tested by such desires, with him or anyone else.

"What did she enjoy?" asked Saric.

"Very little, I think. A bottle of wine in front of the TV, I suppose. She used to dance but had to pack that in after her knee went. The one thing she really did care about was her job. She was a bloody good accountant."

Saric paused him there and instructed Sense Check to re-interpret all references to 'bloody' as 'very', before nodding for Phillip to continue.

"Her clients really loved her. Some of them had been with her for decades."

For the first time, Rob noticed a certain amount of pride in Phillip.

"She wouldn't do my accounts, though, as she said it could be a conflict. She said there were rules against it, and Jane liked a rule." He smiled, and then it was gone. "Anyway, she's been carrying her partner for years, but says she owes him. Sorry, said. Really, she should have forced him out, but I think she just liked having him around, even though she had to clear up after his little mistakes more and more."

"Can we go onto the night in question, please?" said Saric.

"There's really not much to tell. Jane has a conference in Reading. Same place every year. She set off early. It's a two-day thing, so she stays

23

overnight. After that, it was just a normal day for me. I'm on a really big project at the moment and I'm pitching for a stage two. So, I've been spending a lot of time at work. Jane was the same, trying to cram stuff in so she could get out to this conference. Anyway, I couldn't stay out too long because of the bloody dog." (Sense Check flagged a speech pattern anomaly, as it did not recognise what a 'very dog' could be.) "We have a dog walker, but I still have to be back to take it out for an evening walk. So, I get back, have some dinner, and decide to go out on my bike with the dog."

Cyclist. Knew it! thought Rob.

"We went up the bridleway and then I like to cut through the woods in a loop. At this time of year, I can just about get out of the woods again before losing the light. But not this time. We came round a corner and there's a deer right there in the path. Plato, that's the dog, just goes flying off after this thing straight into the woods. And he can really shift, even through undergrowth. A couple of seconds later and they are both just gone. Completely vanished. Normally, if he goes into the woods, I can hear him rustling about somewhere and he is pretty good at finding his way back to me anyway. But not this time. So, I have no choice other than to wander off after him."

Saric paused him again. Sense Check was flagging a need for data. Saric brought up a map on his iPad and handed it to Phillip so that he could make a note of where he thought each of these events had happened. He dropped pins in a number of places. "This is my house; this is where I join the bridleway; this is where I cut off into a track through the woods."

As he added the data, Sense Check allocated some average speeds across the distances and determined a time range for when the dog ran off.

"How long did you look for Plato?" Saric asked.

"Ages. At first, I just went off at random, but I started to get concerned that I wouldn't find my way back to my bike, so then I tried going off in a straight line, making a note of some of the trees as a way to get back. Then I realised this was not a very effective way of covering the area – the dog could have gone anywhere – so I came back to where I started from. So, then I started going along the track instead, which sort of skirts the woods–" he pointed on the screen to the area in question "– and just hoped he would hear me call from there.

"Eventually, I came round a corner, about here I suppose," he added, pointing again, "and he comes bolting out of the woods as if nothing had happened. I reckon I must have been out there for at least two hours. In any case, the last bit of light was just dropping away. Another five minutes and I would have had to give up.

"It was too dark to ride around on dirt tracks by then, so I put Plato on the lead and pushed my bike all the way back home. I didn't get there until *Newsnight* was finishing, so I guess that was about 11.15 pm."

Sense Check requested a start time to run the check across the timing of this trip. Saric asked, and Phillip told him he got home from work at about 7 pm. Sense Check wanted to know what Phillip had for dinner, which was re-heated pasta left over from the previous night. No material impact on timing here. And so they went on for a few minutes, testing and validating various aspects of Phillip's version of events.

By the time they were finished, Saric was content that Phillip's story was consistent and, as Phillip had recognised, very difficult to validate. The police would have checked CCTV records, but Saric knew that CCTV coverage in the quiet leafy corner of West Sussex where Phillip and his wife lived was very limited, other than around the odd corner shop or pub.

"Why didn't you have your phone with you?" asked Rob. He knew they would not be having this conversation at all if Phillip had had it with him that night, as then it would have taken only a few minutes to confirm his location in a dozen different ways.

"It was flat, so I left it on charge," said Phillip.

Rob thought this was odd. He had known many business owners over the years, and the thought of being uncontactable would take every one of them to a state of mild panic.

Saric picked up on this too. "What sort of phone do you have?" he asked.

Phillip told him. As the name of the phone came across the screen, Saric clicked on it and Sense Check pulled up the manufacturer's description, which included claims of a twenty-five-hour battery life for calls. Less for surfing the internet, but how much time would Phillip spend on the internet on his phone whilst at work? Not much, he suspected.

"Did you charge it to full overnight?" asked Saric. Phillip was concentrating hard, and Rob tracked his eyes as they darted from one side to the other whilst he decided how to answer.

"No."

"Why not?"

"I guess I forgot."

"Why didn't you charge it when you got to work, then?"

"Maybe I didn't have a lead, or I just didn't notice it needed doing."

"You can charge your phone to twenty per cent in thirty minutes. Why didn't you charge it whilst you cooked and ate?"

"I suppose I didn't notice it needed doing until it was time to go out."

"At which point it was completely flat?"

Phillip was concentrating again. "Yes," he said.

"So, in the two or three minutes in which you got ready to take the dog out, you first noticed that your phone was flat?" It was not really a question. Saric had had enough. "You recognise, of course, how ridiculous this sounds? I'm not surprised the police are having problems with your explanation of where you were that night. It sounds like you left your phone at home on purpose. Why?"

"This is confidential, right?" asked Phillip.

That depends, thought Saric, but he replied with a yes.

"I wanted a couple of hours to myself. Jane had been banging on at me by text all day, in her breaks I guess, reminding me to get home in time to walk the dog, take out the bins, eat the leftovers. But it was the way she was saying it. She kept saying things like, 'assuming you are alone tonight and have time . . .' In the end I snapped. The last text I sent in reply said something along the lines of, 'If you died, I would manage just fine.'" Phillip had a defiant look to him. "It doesn't mean anything. I was just making a point, but I'm hardly likely to explain that to the police, am I? I deleted my text history, but they can recover that sort of stuff, can't they?"

"Maybe," said Saric.

"Anyway, I'm trying to sell the police a happy marriage, well, as much as I can with my little distraction. I'm hardly likely to tell them I disappeared into the night on my own to get away from my wife's endless bitching on the very evening she ended up being killed. For God's sake, you see that, right?"

"I'm not sure you want to know what I see," said Saric. "However, I accept the case."

"Good," said Phillip.

Rob showed Phillip out. Phillip got into his car, a large black saloon, dialling on his phone as he got into the driver's seat. Something seemed off to Rob; the car looked too clean. Did he really get his car washed whilst his wife's murderer was on the loose and her body was lying somewhere, unburied?

Back in Saric's office, Rob reclined into his preferred seat and had a think. There was much he did not like about the man he had just met, but he knew not to let that get in the way of looking for the truth. There were many ways to deal with the shock of a tragic event. Rob and Saric had met lots of people who had thrown themselves into the mundane to block out the changing reality around them. This did not ring true here, though. Rob did not feel the shattering of true love in Phillip. Perhaps at one time there was something more between him and his wife. In reality, it was hard for Rob to understand that there wouldn't be. He had a great capacity to love, a true, deep, connecting love, that is not universal, and he often found it hard to comprehend people who never found this sort of connection with others. His mind drifted to his own wife. He felt the touch of her hand on his face and saw her eyes looking into his as she raised herself onto tiptoes to kiss him.

"Snap out of it!" demanded Saric, with an impatient tone.

Rob came to with a start and breathed out slowly. "OK, what's next?" he asked.

"Well, his story is coherent in itself, but the whole thing could be rubbish," said Saric. "I'll have a chat with the Deputy Chief and see what he can give us."

CHAPTER 4

Deputy Chief Stephens liked Saric. He recognised that he had an unusually high success rate at unpicking complex cases, and he put it down to him having enough time to focus on one thing at a time. More importantly to the Deputy Chief, he enjoyed Saric's generosity when it came to selecting a good wine, and he found him splendid company at dinner parties and events. The Deputy Chief considered them to share a love of science fiction; novels, obviously, rather than films. Saric would not contradict such a claim, but he actually thought of himself as more of an aficionado than a lover of the genre. So many favours had been exchanged over the years that the Deputy Chief had stopped trying to remember who owed what to whom and just helped Saric out from time to time when he could. He trusted Saric to do the same. Deputy Chief Stephens would draw the line where he saw fit, though. He had a robust sense of public duty and Saric would not push him. For his part, Saric gave away only information – mostly uncovered facts, occasionally strong theories – but never methodologies. As far as Saric knew, the police knew nothing of Sense Check, and their own puny efforts to digitise any area of their work collapsed under the avalanche of bureaucracy and politics associated with any form of public spending. Saric postulated that the better funded and less visible crime agencies must be more advanced in this area, but even here he assumed their efforts would be pointed at mass screening of threats and trends, which was a long way from the individual case targeting he had built Sense Check for.

He could reasonably expect the Deputy Chief to provide some of the key basics of the case. He could also expect him to hold back some of the more interesting features. But that was fine. Saric had many other ways of getting into the detail if he needed to. As he had not needed cash payment for any job since the Dubai situation, he was owed a lot of favours. Unlike the Deputy Chief, Saric kept meticulous records of who owed him what. For now, he kept only a manual record on a spreadsheet. One day, he would look to hardwire this into Sense Check, too, so he would get another angle on where help should come from. For now, he would have to figure that out for himself, with Rob's help.

Rob left Saric to make his calls and went home. He would hit the weights hard that night to help clear his mind and contemplate the next steps for this new case. Guilty or not, if Phillip did go to prison for this, he thought, as he left Saric's house, at least there would be one less cyclist clogging up the roads.

Deputy Chief Stephens sounded relaxed when he answered Saric's call.

Saric got straight to the point. "I wanted to trouble you with a case, if that's OK?"

"Yes, yes, no problem. Hang on a sec." Saric heard voices in the background, a bar perhaps, but a respectable one.

I bet he's at the golf club, thought Saric.

"That's better. Right, what can I do for you?"

"We've picked up the Jane Evans case. Her husband hired us."

"Interesting. Look, I can give you a few pointers on that, but first I need some help from you."

"OK." Saric's hands hovered over his keyboard ready to make a note of the favour. "What can I do for you?"

"I've finally ploughed through that dreadful series my wife recommended to me. It had bloody dragons in it, Saric. Why do people get so sucked into this stuff? So, now I can 'talk about the relationships' in the story with Mrs Stephens, but more importantly, I can read something decent at last. So, come on, give me a recommendation."

"OK." Saric's hands dropped and he sat back in his chair. This felt like a lot of responsibility. He read novels to learn about the world, about people, about himself. He did not read exclusively science fiction but would not go too many books before coming back to it. From long, half-drunk discussions, he knew the Deputy Chief read to escape, and for fun. It was interesting to Saric that although they were reading for different reasons, they managed to enjoy the same books.

Despite being very well read in the genre, the Deputy Chief liked to get stuck into series of books. Something substantial he could get into. He had gaps in the classics. Saric thought about the times they were living in. A world where lies became truth by popular opinion. Where experts were rejected as irrelevant if they disagreed with you. Where fat, useless people assumed they were superior to those who worked hard their whole lives, just on the basis of where they were born. A few books came to mind, and one in particular seemed to speak to this world.

"Have you read *Fahrenheit 451*?" Saric asked.

"No. Good, is it?"

"Yes."

"I'll give it a go, then. Thanks. Now, what do you want to know about this case?"

It was an unnecessary question. Deputy Chief Stephens knew Saric wanted to know everything, and Saric knew he would be told as much as the Deputy Chief felt comfortable with. So, they discussed the case, whilst Saric made notes.

CHAPTER 5

The following day, Saric filled Rob in on what he had managed to uncover from a couple of hours on the phone the previous evening.

At 10.15 am, Jane Evans, aged 48, was found dead in a soulless hotel in Reading by the cleaning staff. The time of death was estimated to be somewhere around midnight the previous evening. She had been suffocated with a pillow. There was no sign of forced entry, indicating she knew her attacker. She was wearing normal bed clothes. There was no sign of anyone else being in the room with her for the evening. All of this Saric got from Deputy Chief Stephens. Some subsequent calls, as he cashed in favours from other police officers whose careers he had helped, added further information. These officers were not directly involved in the case, but they had picked up some of the details from colleagues. No unaccountable DNA had been recovered from the scene. The pillow used to smother the victim had a wet patch on it – some sort of fluid, but not sick or blood. The people in the neighbouring rooms heard nothing, albeit one of them did not get to their room until about 1.30 am, so they may have missed the whole thing, and the other confessed to being "pretty wasted". Jane herself had been drinking. This probably explained why hotel records showed that she lost her room key during the evening and had it replaced after the conference.

She was an accountant, as Phillip had told them. No criminal record; not even a speeding ticket. Business seemed to be going well, and there were no signs of any significant debts. There were no issues in and around her family life to speak of. No easily accessed threatening emails, texts or social media posts at home or work. They were waiting for the paperwork to clear before having a poke around for anything they could recover from deleted work or home texts and emails, but they were not expecting much to come from that.

Phillip was right that they had him at the centre stage for their investigation. The statistics said he was the most likely candidate and his alibi was weak. The only criminal activity anywhere near Jane was her business partner, Tony, who twenty years ago had been caught up in an investigation over low-level fraud. But nothing ever stuck to him and it didn't become public.

Sense Check had also pulled all the media coverage it could find. The murder had not received much attention. Whilst the victim was a white middle-class woman, which would normally have gained good traction in the press, the only angle that would have given it enough spice to really get going as a national story was one that the police had kept back from reporters on the basis it may prove useful in future interrogations. Despite Saric's efforts, it had been kept back from him, too. The local press was not really geared up for murders, so it got a mention, but significantly fewer words were dedicated to it than the monstrous suggestion of a new, 7,000-home estate that had been lodged with the planning department, which, of course, had to be stopped.

Saric had populated Sense Check with the data and, building on the exchange with Phillip, a number of issues were troubling him.

Above all was the odd business with the phones. Phillip must have known that deleting his text history would not stop the police finding it on his wife's phone. Unless he had deleted it himself, of course. But the police had not picked up on this exchange, so Jane must have deleted it, too, or it never happened. This was unsatisfactory.

Sense Check was also firing out a series of incomplete fact patterns from the data it had been given. Different forms of attack should bring with them certain types of evidence. When someone is suffocated, they should struggle. There should be noise and physical evidence on the victim, such as bruises or cuts. But no one heard anything, and it seemed Jane did not fight back. And the liquid on the pillow was perplexing. He would have to follow that up later for an explanation.

Phillip's explanation of what he was doing that night did, however, hang together. The deer population in the South Downs was thriving. The route was described in some detail and the timings worked. He might get one of his boys to cycle the route for completeness, but this was not top of the list of actions.

Rob listened to Saric's update with a deep level of concentration. He enjoyed the precise way Saric spoke. Since working with Saric, Rob's social circle had become much smaller, and he often found that the waffling nature of small talk irritated him, even though he remained perfectly accomplished at it.

"Why are you taking this one?" Rob asked.

Saric looked a little surprised by the question

"And don't bullshit me with nonsense about justice, or a greater good."

"Phillip was a referral. The referral market is important. If we turn too many away it will dry up. Anyway, it seems at least possible it wasn't him, in which case I'm intrigued to know who managed to get excited enough by this seemingly innocuous woman to end up killing her."

"Maybe she wasn't innocuous," Rob said out of instinct, knowing they were a long way from really taking a view on this one way or another.

"How about," said Saric, "we start from the premise that it wasn't Phillip? Where else in her life could she have developed a connection with someone capable of building to this?"

"In order," Rob said, "family, lover, friends, work, random exchange with a nutter."

Saric thought on that for a moment. "Family; I agree, that's worth a look. If she had a lover, I doubt she would have been giving her husband such a hard time about his. Friendship rarely generates enough emotional leverage to result in premeditated, non-sexual, violent crime. Work, agreed. If we end up pursuing the random nutter theory, I give up.

"As for family," he went on, "I suggest we let the police do the hard yards; they are starting there anyway. I think that leaves us with work."

"In which case, we are going to need an accountant on board. Unless you're hiding that skillset in your weird history?" said Rob.

"Not a clue," admitted Saric. "Who have we got?"

They reviewed the favours-owed files and, as they started thinning down those who could be useful, they arrived at the obvious candidate. As he saw her face in the picture again, Rob smiled. Grace Simone. Quirky did not really cover it. She had a fearsome energy and a bright mind that never travelled in quite the same direction as anyone else in the room. She was a petite woman, which made it even more enjoyable to see her fill a room. She was a trained accountant, albeit she had since moved from accounting to corporate financing, then onto strategic advice and now charged multinational companies the price of a small car for a day's work resolving board-level disagreements. But what Rob liked most about her was the effect she had on Saric. She was not classically beautiful, but she could shoot a look that would make you fall in love in an instant and then immediately pull it away. Rob very much hoped she would be able to help.

Saric put her name into Sense Check, which quickly confirmed she was in the UK and still working, before providing contact details. To Rob's mind, she still looked exactly the same, even though five years had passed since they had recovered her from a bad business situation that had got as far as death threats. Saric's response had been rather more brutal than he would usually have allowed, but it had certainly worked. They had never called on her to settle the debt since.

"You call her," suggested Saric. Rob smiled.

Rob managed to navigate Grace's PA to get an urgent message through to her. He only had to wait twenty minutes for the call back. Saric watched, frustrated to be hearing only one half of the conversation, but Rob made a point of pretending not to think to put the call on speaker. He made arrangements to meet locally for breakfast the next morning.

"Yes, Saric will be there . . ." he said, raising an eyebrow at his old friend.

"Screw you," Saric mouthed back.

"That gives us a day to play with. Crime scene?" asked Rob.

CHAPTER 6

Having agreed on a visit to the crime scene, they drove off to Reading. Saric argued for the motorway route, but as Rob was driving, he overruled him for the less mind-numbing but equally excruciating task of moving east to west on the roads of West Sussex, Surrey and, eventually, Berkshire. If Phillip had driven out to kill his wife, he would surely have come this way to try and avoid the motorway traffic cameras. As they trudged along the dual carriageways, Saric thought it seemed a long way for a man to go to kill his wife. Maybe he went there for some other reason?

They travelled mostly in silence. Although Saric could be quite sociable in the right setting, when his mind was on a case, he liked to stay focused and did not tolerate idle gossiping, even with Rob. One side effect of Saric's dislike of unnecessary chatter was that more of their time was spent in silence than might be considered normal in any other friendship. This suited Rob, though; it gave him time to think, and he didn't always want Saric to know what was on his mind.

After a couple of hours, Saric interrupted Rob's thoughts to ask that they go to the conference centre before visiting the hotel. Rob did not know Reading well and it took a few attempts to navigate the complex one-way system before they found the venue. It was the weekend now, so any accounting banners that may have been up three days previously had been replaced by those promoting a wedding fair. They used the fact that this event was open to the public to take a look around. Although the set up was completely different to how it would have been for the accounting conference, they both found it useful to be in the space. For Rob, this was because it gave him a feel for the atmosphere, while Saric was seeking out more data in case it came to be useful later.

"What an awful place to spend any time at all," said Rob. "Most of these rooms don't even have windows for fresh air or natural light. I feel like I'm in some sort of underground maze built to turn its occupants slowly insane."

Saric had noticed the lack of light, but only registered its miserable effect when Rob pointed it out. "Yes," he agreed, "if Dante was writing his *Inferno* today, this would surely have been the setting for one circle of hell."

Even the young couples milling around pondering bridal gowns could not lift the mood. All around were mums fussing and giving almost exclusively inappropriate recommendations, while dads desperately tried not to mention the couple's budget in every sentence. The gloom of the setting seemed to suck out any joy from blossoming, everlasting love, replacing it with just another chance to consume.

After less than an hour, sensing that there was nothing more to be learned at the conference centre, they moved on to the hotel, which was a short way out on the other side of town. Rob thought it strange that Jane had not chosen one of the many town centre hotels, which were in walking distance of the conference.

"Parking," Saric pointed out, "expensive and limited, or not available at all."

Saric had already checked; the journey from Jane Evans's house to Reading on public transport was not a straightforward one.

•

The hotel had two floors and carried the branding of a national chain. It was like any number of other hotels across the country, which was reassuring for guests, if not exciting. Outside the entrance to the hotel itself was a second door that led to a small restaurant and bar area. Saric had already established that Jane had attended a dinner at the conference before returning to her hotel in a taxi with a couple of other delegates. They had enjoyed a few more drinks in the bar before going to bed.

Saric stepped into the hotel reception, which was little more than a small hallway with a large counter along one side. The receptionist was on the phone dealing with what sounded like a complaint. He mouthed an apology while making a sort of shrugging motion, to emphasise that the delay was not his fault. Saric didn't mind at all. He used the time to consider his surroundings; at the other end of the reception corridor was another door that required a pass to open. He assumed that would be operated by a hotel room key. There were then two floors of rooms set either side of a long corridor. Saric knew there would be fire escapes at the other end of those corridors, connected to automatic alarms.

The receptionist finished his call and apologised for the wait. One of the most difficult things about the work that Rob and Saric did was requesting information without the same rights the police have. Early on in their partnership, Rob had agreed with Saric that they would never impersonate the police in order to get information. In pursuit of his new career, Rob did not want to give up his moral code entirely. Impersonating the police is just not right. Saric was generally more relaxed about the moral underpinning of the law, and he had never been convinced that there was actually a right and wrong at all, but Rob's value to his work was worth the little sacrifice of holding a firmer line on the legality of his practices, at least when they were working on a job together.

In any case, Saric had found that most people were happy to talk, and this was particularly true when Rob was asking the questions.

"Hi Peter – that is your badge I assume – that sounded painful." Rob gestured to the phone.

"Ha, we get used to it."

Rob guessed the young man was somewhere around twenty. He was skinny, with long, shaggy hair. His teeth were not well looked after. Rob found young men this age hard work. Already, Peter looked to be losing interest. On the plus side, Rob would bet on this being Peter's main income source. He did not look like a student on a break. If Peter was not forthcoming, that might be all Rob needed.

"We are private detectives. We have been hired by the husband of the woman who was murdered here."

"I don't know anything about that. I wasn't working that night. The police have been all over it; the room and everyone that was on that day."

"Yes, and we don't need to replicate any of that, thanks. We just have a slightly different way of working, so it's useful for us to see things for ourselves."

"Fair enough. Do you want me to get the manager on duty?"

"No, I don't think we need to bother them, thanks. What would be great is to just pop into the room. Just for a moment."

"Ha. Yeah, right. Look, I don't really care who you are, but we've been told about journalists poking around. Or weirdos. We're not supposed to say anything, and this might be a crappy little job, but it's easy and I like it. So, seriously, if you don't mind . . ." He nodded towards the door.

"OK. And good for you. You should be careful. But it would really benefit our investigation to see the crime scene; it gives us context. Maybe we could make it easier for you to help us out?" Rob pulled out his wallet as he spoke. "This is a minimum wage job, right? What's that, twelve quid an hour? A bit more? How about you do a week's work in the next twenty minutes?"

That sounded about right to Rob, but it left him with some mental maths that was beyond him to calculate without losing his train of thought.

Saric saw the moment of confusion on Rob's face. "£420," he suggested, calculating a working week as 35 hours, which he must have heard from somewhere because he had never had a job where it mattered.

"Call it £450," said Rob.

"Are you two for real?"

Rob took the cash out of his wallet. "Yes," he said.

"Fine, but if anyone finds out, I'm going to tell them you made me do it."

He took a key card from a drawer, did something on the computer, swiped the card through a machine and gestured for them to follow him.

"It was room twenty-seven. I wasn't here that night, but I came on at lunch the day after. The police were in there all day, and some of the following one. They took the body, some of the sheets and pillows, and most of her stuff, but they left us to clear up. None of the cleaners would go near it, so head office sorted out a specialist team. Apparently, they get a lot of work from hotels. It's gross. Loads of suicides. You know we charged her account for the clean-up? Ha. What a job. Couple of right geezers they were. They knew what they were doing. You would never have known, they just looked like a couple of heating engineers. In the end, we didn't even change the sodding mattress! Not enough blood on it apparently, so they cleaned it and that was that."

The corridor was decorated in an off-brown wallpaper and the carpet was a swirl of dark grey and dark yellow that reminded Rob of old photos of his grandparents' house. The colours seemed to be selected purely on the basis of what combination was best able to absorb stains. No attempt had been made to make the place look nice. It was simply functional. It smelled clean, though.

They got to the door. Peter looked up and down the corridor, as if it was not too late to explain what he was doing, and then opened the door. He let Rob and Saric go in first and then stepped into the room and let the door shut.

It looked like any other hotel room in this or any rival chain. The bed was made. The generic hotel furniture was in all the right places. A mirror, a TV, a desk chair, a side chair, a digital clock, a desk phone, a plastic tray with neatly arranged tea bags and coffee granules, and a slightly too small kettle. Rob knew that with a determined search he would also find a hair dryer somewhere. There was no sign of anything untoward. Despite this, Rob thought there was a strange feeling hanging in the room, but he was sure he was creating it from what he knew had happened here. He looked down at the bed. There was just nothing special about this place. In a few days, when head office felt sure the story was not going to go national, they would re-open the room and someone would rest their head happily down on the pillows and sleep soundly.

Saric took it all in, then walked back to the door and took a few steps forward to where he could see the bed. He paused there, then walked around the bed until he was standing right next to it. He picked up a pillow, squeezed it, and put it back. He knelt down on the floor and took a close look at the carpet. It had been cleaned.

"Nothing more from me," he said to Rob. Rob nodded.

On the way back down the stairs, Saric asked, "I assume you have CCTV around the place?"

"Ha, yeah, you could say that," Peter sniggered. "You should ask the cops about that. They don't spend money here unless they have to. I haven't seen it, but I doubt anyone's going down off the footage from those old things."

Saric looked at Rob. They were both thinking the same thing. This had not helped at all.

CHAPTER 7

EARLY JULY 2015

The sun was hot on her pale skin, which had forgotten the ferocity of its rays here in the longest days of the year. She should have waited. A few more weeks and the weather would have been cooler; it might have been easier.

But she could not wait. She did not know when another opportunity would arise, and she had to protect him.

It had been reckless to try, and she could not afford to be reckless. Not while they had him. They would not hurt him; she was certain of that. He was what they wanted, the reason why they had gone to such lengths and taken so many risks to get them here after all these years. If she could get out, somewhere safe, she could get help.

She remembered how it was last time. The careful planning over many months and the sacrifices others made. This time was different; she had to protect him before everything else. So, she had to try now.

She felt every rock through the thin soles of the shoes they had given her. The men had made her change before reaching the compound. When she was young, she had enjoyed dressing like all the other girls, as she had felt part of something. Now the dull dress caught around her ankles as she ran, and the tight collar pulled at her neck as her tiring lungs grasped for more air.

As she passed over the rocky terrain, she struggled to stay on her feet, although she was barely aware of it and focused only on getting as far away as she could.

This far from the town, the roads were not much more than tracks. Following their path was a risk, but she could not chance moving too far away and into thousands of miles of rocky hills. If she moved away from the tracks, she would be lost and she could not risk being unable to get back to him.

The leaders had cars, which allowed the most trusted to leave for essential visits to get food and supplies. Those cars had saved her once but now they were coming for her.

She stopped, as she had done every few minutes for what seemed like hours since she had finally gathered the courage to leave the compound through a small gap in the fence. Over the pounding of her pulse, which seemed to move through every part of her body, she listened for the tell-tale sound of an engine. Someone must be searching for her by now.

Silence. There was nothing but the sound of a few birds slowly circling overhead. It was never this quiet at home. At home she never felt away from everything like she had here. But she had been away for nearly as long as she had lived here as a child. She was a different person now, and she knew what it felt like to be safe. At least she thought so.

She could not afford to stop for long, even though her legs were shaking from running. She had thought she was fit, but weekly sessions with her personal trainer and runs in the park at home had not prepared her for this. The ground was uneven and unforgiving. And she was running for her life.

From nowhere, she heard the murmur of an engine and cursed herself for not getting farther from the road. For a moment, she thought about running, but it was too open here. They would see her, and if they saw her, they would catch her.

She looked around for somewhere that might hide her for long enough that they would move on. Briefly, she wondered how they had known which way she had gone. Perhaps they had more than one team looking, or maybe it was just luck. It did not matter now. They were here and she had to hide.

She pressed herself into a small opening in the side of a hill and hoped that they would not look too closely as they passed. At times like this, she wished she could believe the way they did, that there was some higher power who might help her. But there was only her, alone, thousands of miles from home.

They were getting close now and she could feel the vibrations from the car moving slowly down the dusty road. She tried to quieten her breathing, even though she knew they would not hear her over the sound of the engine. They were not moving fast enough. She could tell that now. And the car was slowing as it approached. Gently, in no hurry, the car rolled to a stop close to the rocks.

The door clicked open and a pair of worn leather boots swung out and crushed the gravel under them. The man was heavy, and he groaned slightly as he pulled himself through the door before stretching, as if he had been stuck in the car for a while.

With a calmness matching her panic, he walked towards her. Instinctively, but knowing it was useless, she pulled herself closer towards the rock, hoping it might shield her. But it was too late.

His large body blocked her exit and he loomed over her as he whispered, "Hello, Martha, where do you think you're going?"

CHAPTER 8

It was late by the time they got back to Sussex and they had an early start the next day. This was not a problem or particularly unusual, as neither man slept very much. They were waiting in the restaurant the next morning when Grace walked in. She had been late for every meeting that they had ever had, so this was no exception. Usually this type of behaviour would have made Saric short tempered, as he viewed time spent waiting as time wasted. Rob suspected that a combination of Grace's striking looks, her engaging personality, and the fact that she had inevitably been dealing with an incredibly important business matter meant that he overlooked her poor timekeeping in a way that he might not have done for others.

The owner of the café was an old contact of Saric's who was always happy to find them a quiet table where they could discuss cases. Later in the day, the place would become busier with people meeting for coffee or brunch and the occasional business meeting, but at the moment they were the only customers.

Grace appeared outside the café. She was distracted by the phone call she was in the middle of. She stood for a moment in fierce concentration and then relaxed, looked inside the café, noticed Saric and Rob at the only occupied table and bustled in.

As soon as she made it through the door, her attention returned to her phone call. "I appreciate you are a Lord, but is it really necessary for everyone to use your full title at private meetings? I'm sure you can see how irritating that gets for your colleagues."

Rob and Saric exchanged looks and waited patiently for Grace to wrap things up.

Grace smiled at the woman behind the counter and gave a little wave. Without making any effort to mute the phone, she asked, "May I have a black coffee, a big one, please. They are paying."

Then she turned and looked at Rob and Saric, as if making some sort of calculation. Her phone was still at her ear. "I'm sorry, but I'm going to have to pick this up with you later. I really don't think you should press this today, though. Let me talk it through with you first. I would not want you to misjudge where the loyalties lie in the organisation right now. Yes,

yes. OK, I'll try." She hung up. "Well, this place is cute. You two look tired. How are you both?"

Rob, expecting Saric to say something, left a slightly unnatural pause, which Saric failed to fill.

"Bit early for you?" Grace laughed. "Well, you always were one for getting straight down to business, Saric."

"Yes, we are both fine, thank you," said Rob.

Saric agreed. "It's great to see you," he said. "We were both pleased to hear you could help."

"That was the deal, right?"

"Busy morning already by the looks of it," said Rob.

"Just one little thing to clear out the diary. He's going to be 'Lord Sacked' by the end of the week if he doesn't pay attention. Some people can't be helped."

Grace's coffee arrived. Saric introduced her to the owner, who had brought it over. "Anything to eat?" she asked.

"The coffee will do for now, thanks. It all looks amazing, though," she added, so as not to hurt the owner's feelings.

"Let's see if there's time to catch up later in the day. First, fill me in so I can repay this debt."

For someone who was usually concise in his delivery, Saric seemed a little unsure in how he explained the background facts of the case, as if he was rather too keen to ensure that Grace did not think he had missed anything. This was unlike Saric, who rarely felt the need to demonstrate his credentials to others, and it amused Rob to watch him second guess his own delivery.

Grace listened carefully to Saric, but she did not interrupt him with any questions while he spoke. Instead, she appeared to be committing as much detail as possible to memory, so that it would be available to her later, if and when it was needed. Watching her, Rob could see that her ability to assess and utilise information would be a great asset to them on this case, perhaps even more so than her accounting knowledge. While he valued Sense Check greatly, there were still connections that required a human mind, and Grace clearly had a great one, and one which Saric might just listen to.

When Saric had finished, Grace outlined how high street accountancy firms work. "It's all about how many hours you spend on a particular project. Each individual will charge a certain price per hour for their time, which will be billed to the client.

"At a place like that, most of the business will come from referrals, with a heavy emphasis on personal relationships between the partners and their clients. Sometimes the advice is technical in nature; what deductions can be taken for expenses and that sort of thing, but most of that would usually be dealt with by junior employees. For experienced practitioners like Jane and her partner, more time will be spent giving strategic advice about the future of the business and solving problems."

"We've asked for access to her work emails and phone records. Is there anything else we should be looking for?" asked Rob

"I'd get her time sheets, too, that's where she would have recorded what she was working on." She hesitated slightly, as if weighing up whether she really wanted to pursue a particular line of conversation, before adding, "but none of this will make any sense to you; you'll need someone who understands accounting to unpick all the jargon."

"That's where you come in," Saric said, with a slight note of apprehension in his voice that Rob had not heard before. "When we get the data, we will ask you to review it for us, to interpret any technical areas and give us your analysis of the situation."

"I can do better than that," interrupted Grace quickly. "When my PA said that you wanted to see me, I thought it might be time to repay my debt to you, so I have cleared my schedule today. It would be better for me to come with you, to meet the partner – at least I assume that is where you intend to go next – that way I can ask the questions that need to be asked, instead of relying on you to notice the right things."

Saric smiled broadly; he had been hoping she might offer this.

While they finished their drinks, they discussed the finer details of the case and reviewed the areas of uncertainty that needed to be resolved. Before they left to travel to the accountancy office, Rob couldn't resist asking one more question; partly because he was enjoying the conversation and partly because he knew it was the kind of speculative question that Saric would never ask. "Grace, no offence, but accountants have a reputation for being, sort of, well . . . boring." Grace raised an eyebrow and gave Rob a look that reminded him that she was never boring. "In general, I mean." He was slightly flustered now but pursued his line of inquiry. "Is it really possible that someone could be driven to murder someone over an accounting matter?"

Grace looked straight at him to answer. "The thing you need to remember is that this type of accountant will be dealing with many aspects of a person's life, both in business and personal matters, so they can get quite close. In some cases, they will know things that their client's family don't even know. So yes, I'd say there could be enough to drive someone to kill."

Rob called Tony Spencer of Spencer and Evans Accountants. Tony was happy enough to meet them, as a courtesy to Jane's husband, for whom he seemed to have a genuine sense of sympathy. He said he would see them right away.

CHAPTER 9

In the few days since Jane's death, the office of Spencer and Evans Accountants had become a scene of chaos. Tony was starting to understand just how much Jane had been carrying him in recent years, in all aspects of the practice, including the general running of the office. Rob, Saric and Grace were shown into Tony's office by a well presented, heavy chested middle-aged receptionist, who was working hard to maintain a superior tone. Rob smiled his most charming smile at her, got no reaction, then, remembering her boss had just been murdered and she was probably worrying about the continued existence of her job, regretted it.

Tony's office was a mess. Rob had imagined something grander. In fact, the furniture was cheap; there was an obviously plastic plant in the corner, and no pictures on the walls. There were a couple of frames on the desk, but Rob couldn't see the pictures inside, as they were facing Tony. Wife and kids, he assumed.

Tony was a big man, albeit out of shape now. Rob watched with interest as the handshake ritual began. Tony came around his desk to

Rob first – a well-practiced handshake Rob observed – then walked past Grace to Saric. Finally, he bent forward slightly, as if he were about to explain something complicated to a child, and shook Grace's hand.

Oh dear, thought Rob.

The nice to meet yous were exchanged, as well as a short expression of sympathy for Tony's loss, before they got to the point of their visit.

"Grace is a consultant providing us advice on this case. She has an understanding of your line of business," explained Saric. "We appreciate you have spent time with the police already, but we do not pursue cases using the same approach. I may need to take notes as we speak–" he nodded at his laptop– "I assume that's fine with you?"

Sense Check fired up, and Saric turned on the voice recognition program.

"We are trying to get an understanding of the sort of work Jane did here, and the people she has been spending time with recently," said Saric.

He turned to look at Grace, who was sitting very upright, her eyes fixed on Tony. "Can you describe your client base?" she asked.

Tony looked at her, as if he had only just noticed she was in the room.

"Well, we provide advice to people about financial matters. You see, when someone runs a business, they sell things and that's their income, and they have to pay for things, too. For example, their staff. That's their costs. So, they need to keep a track of the money coming in and going out, and they . . ."

"For pity's sake, man, we're going to have to go a bit faster than that!" Grace laughed. "Let's just imagine that I know more about the world of business than twenty Tony Spencers, and try this again. What sort of clients do you have here? Is it all corporate or do you do private client wealth, too? Do you have any specialisms? That sort of thing."

Tony looked at Grace with surprise, then turned back to Rob before starting his explanation. "We provide a range of accounting services across a broad client base. Most of our clients run their own businesses, so we advise both the business and the owners in things like tax and estate planning, as well as drawing up accounts and things like that. Most of my clients have been with me for years. Some of them are doing very well for themselves, so we get lots of referrals from their contacts."

"What about Jane? What did she do?" Grace pressed on, ignoring Tony's clear preference for dealing with Rob.

"Jane and I have worked together for a long time; I took her on as a trainee twenty years ago and she never left. I guess you could say I've been a sort of mentor to her over the years, and she eventually joined me in the partnership. It's good to have a woman around, helps business, some clients like that sort of thing."

Grace sat a little straighter, but before she could interrupt, Tony hastily added, "She was good, though, really earned her place here."

Looking around the chaotic office, Rob suspected Jane might have needed rather less support from Tony than he was implying. Grace looked similarly unconvinced but carried on with her questions without testing the mismatch between Tony's view of Jane and where all the evidence pointed.

After some prompting, Tony described how business had never been better, with no money worries. Saric raised an eyebrow at this point, when Sense Check flagged that this was not supported by the partnership's accounts. The business was profitable but had been steadily declining over the last few years.

Tony also explained that Jane's specialism was tax and her clients were across a wide range of industries. "She had a particular interest in charities. I never could understand why she bothered with them. No money in charity, is there? But it kept her happy, so I never really stopped her."

Over the next hour, Rob and Saric witnessed Grace utilise all her professional skills to grill Tony on his firm. She had not been wrong when she stated that she knew far more about business than him, and while Tony was careful to project an image of the successful businessman ruling over a small empire, Grace's precise and persistent questioning gradually drew out a picture of a man who had given up a long time ago and was coasting towards retirement on the hard work of others. Most of that hard work appeared to have been Jane's, and it was easy to see that things had become strained between them in recent months.

Rob was pleased that Grace chose to pursue this area a little further, stepping away from the specific accounting remit they had given her.

"Were the two of you ever anything more than colleagues?" she asked.

Tony snapped his reply. "Of course not. No, nothing like that. She would never have done it, never liked to break any rules. She was too loyal to that husband of hers. Have you met him? He's the one you should be looking at. Running around with another woman. Did you know that?"

"We are not the police, we are just trying to find out what happened," Saric said calmly. He had been unusually quiet while Grace had led the conversation, but he had lost patience with Tony. "We would now like to have a look round Jane's office. Please can you arrange for us to be provided with the passwords for her computer?"

"Absolutely not! Those files are confidential! There's no way that can happen."

If Saric was surprised by this reaction he didn't let it show and calmly carried on. "Mr Spencer, we are simply here to find out what happened to Jane. We have no interest in any other matter. If you had nothing to do with Jane's murder, then there is no reason not to let us see the files. At the moment, the police have no interest in you, but that could change at any time, and I expect they would have more interest than us in any other matters they discover while reviewing your files."

Saric held Tony's gaze for several seconds, during which time Rob wondered what silent negotiation was going on between the two men. He looked at Grace to seek some explanation, but she was giving nothing away.

Eventually, Tony sighed and gave way. "OK," he said, "my secretary can give you access, tell her I authorised it."

"Thank you, Mr Spencer, we appreciate your help."

The look on Tony's face indicated that he did not appreciate being asked to provide it, but nevertheless he nodded politely.

"Finally, Mr Spencer, can you tell us what your movements were on the evening of Tuesday the 16th of June?" Saric asked this as if it were a routine question, but even he was not able to resist the briefest of glances towards his computer screen, where Sense Check was waiting to receive the data.

"You can't think I had anything to do with this? That's ridiculous! I told the police—"

"As I said, Mr Spencer, we are not the police, but we do need to know, so that we can eliminate you, if that is appropriate."

"I was at a dinner at the golf club. They run them once a month for important businessmen in the town. It's a sort of networking thing, and I get a lot of good business from it. I know it was that day because it gave me a good excuse not to go to the conference. Those things are so boring, they're like torture."

His voice trailed off as he remembered the context of their conversation.

After a brief pause, he started again. "I got a taxi from the office to the club at about 6.30 pm, I guess. My secretary could confirm that, as she booked it, and I was there until gone 1 am, when I got another taxi back home. Those things always get a bit boozy, so I don't take the car."

Saric was pleased. Attendance at that kind of event should be easy to verify, with lots of reliable, independent witnesses; interactions with attendees and staff and taxi records that could confirm the times.

"Did Mrs Evans ever attend the dinners, if they are so good for business?" Saric continued. Perhaps this was another avenue to explore, some unhappy acquaintance with a score to settle.

Tony looked at Saric blankly for a moment, as if this was a strange question. "No, as I said before, these are networking events for local businessmen, so they wouldn't interest Jane. The only women there are the girls who serve the drinks and food."

They thanked Tony and the same receptionist showed them into Jane's office, which was on the other side of the reception from Tony's. Although it contained the same cheap furniture, the room could not have been more different. The desk was neat, and orderly bookshelves contained a series of reference books. There were three certificates on the wall, each demonstrating a particular professional qualification, which Jane had obtained two decades earlier. The only personal item on Jane's desk was a photo of her and her dog.

The receptionist gave Grace access to Jane's computer and filing cabinet, and she spent the next hour methodically working through her emails and notes.

During this time, Rob and Saric reviewed Sense Check's output in a little more detail than they could in real time. Much of the conversation had been flagged as requiring further data. This surprised neither man, as Tony's projection of his own self-image was clearly far from the reality.

Sense Check suggested further work was required on the slowdown in business, and Saric asked Grace to focus on this area, alongside looking at Jane's client work.

It was past the end of the working day by the time they were finished. The staff had left on the dot of 5.30 pm and only Tony and the receptionist were left by 6 pm, when Grace finally announced she had enough of a view of the business to call it a day.

The three of them walked back to Tony's office to let him know they were off, but he was busy with a client. They lingered outside in silence. Tony had left the door open and they caught some of the conversation before they were noticed.

"What the hell are you doing letting a bunch of snoops into the books, are you completely insane?" A broad set young man was looming over Tony, who was sitting at his desk. He was wearing a dark, fashionable suit, which did not seem to be in keeping with the rest of his appearance. Rob thought he would have been more at home in a tracksuit. "Jim is going to do his nut," the man added.

"Don't worry about it, they are only looking at Jane's system. They can't access any of my client records. You know I know how to look after Jim. I've never let you down, have I?

"Jane's husband has hired them, so I've got to give them something, haven't I–" he noticed his guests and stopped.

"All done, are we?" he said, trying to recover his superior tone in front of the threatening-looking man in his office.

The young man's blood was up, and he was standing with his legs apart and his chest out. He glared at Rob, Saric and Grace.

"I think we have what we need for now," said Grace. She looked up at the young man. "Is there something I can do for you?" she asked. She was completely calm, and her tone reminded Rob of a seen-it-all before teacher addressing the latest iteration of a school bully. "You're all puffed up like a cockerel on heat," she added.

The young man seemed ill equipped to manage the situation. Some sort of internal moral code was telling him you should not intimidate a woman, but if a man had said that to him his solution would be obvious. Rob could see he was confused.

"You need to shut your mouth," was all he could muster. "And what do you think you're looking at?" he added, directing his question at Saric. They could all feel the tension. Tony was frozen to the spot.

It was in Rob's nature to avoid conflict, and he was not quick to anger. Managing this sort of situation was something that he had learned. Although of average height, he had become a very strong man through sport and training. He had a soft face, though, and would never look intimidating to this type of man. Saric, on the other hand, was taller and broader than his friend, and although less muscular, he looked like he was carved from granite. And when in a conflict, his eyes looked dead, incapable of sympathy. Or mercy.

He took a step forward and closed the gap between him and his aggressor to within range of a strike. The young man was not used to his challenges being accepted these days. Didn't this guy know who he was? Saric was silent, but he held the man's gaze. Rob was not really expecting a reaction from Saric; he would not normally be bothered by this sort of low-level thuggery, but it was sort of reassuring to know that even Saric could become a little clouded by his more primitive emotions from time to time.

"Pack it in," said Grace. "I've got better things to do with my time than this. The world is full of morons, and we're not going to change that with all this posturing."

Saric took a step back, and Grace placed a hand on his arm.

"Thank you, Tony," said Rob, "time for us to go." And they left.

"That was a bit odd," said Rob, once they were outside. "I guess Tony is not as clean as he might like to seem."

"Let's get something to eat," said Grace, "and Saric, you can buy me a nice glass of wine. Then I will tell you what I think."

CHAPTER 10

LATE JULY 2015

They had taken her to a small room on the third floor. The final flight of stairs was uneven where the heavy wood had worn away through decades of footsteps and polishing. The ceiling was too high for the narrow room, which was once part of a much larger room and now partitioned into a row of narrow bedrooms.

She sat on the edge of a narrow, single bed. The only other furniture in the room was a wooden desk, painted white many years ago, and a rickety wooden chair. Two small shelves held a few personal items and a single book.

She had been in the room for three nights now. She'd received no visitors, except for a matronly woman who brought her food and water three times a day. The room was clean and, if not as comfortable as her cosy cottage, at least she was safe.

She was not a prisoner in any normal sense; there were no locks on the door, and no one had told her that she couldn't leave. But their meaning was clear enough.

"We trusted you and this is how you choose to show gratitude."

"This is what happens when you are exposed to dangerous influence."

So, she remained in the room, marking the passage of time through the changing light coming through the tiny window, which opened just enough to let the weak summer breeze attempt to cool the cramped space. They had left the window unlocked, but it didn't matter, as she was too high up to jump, and anyway, where would she go? Running was no longer an option.

As the light was fading on the third day, the heavy man who had found her appeared at her door. He knocked roughly but entered before she had a chance to answer. Privacy was not a high priority here. If you required privacy it meant you had something to hide, and secrets were not tolerated.

The man indicated that she should follow him, and she stepped hesitantly into the corridor.

Around her, other women were moving between rooms in silence, and with their heads down, not meeting her eye. At another time, she might have wondered about their stories, but for now her mind was filled with hundreds of possibilities for where she was being taken and how she might respond to each one.

At the foot of the final flight of stairs, the man knocked on a heavy wooden door. Getting no response, he opened it and ushered her through.

As she stepped into the room, her eyes settled on the thing she had hoped most to see. In the corner, playing with a wooden model of a horse, was a wide-eyed, dark-haired boy.

"Ollie!" she exclaimed, breaking into a run towards him. His eyes lit up as he saw her, but before she could reach him a shadow moved across the carpet and a familiar face interrupted her.

"Before you do that, we have some things to discuss."

She turned to her right. Standing between her and the boy was an old couple.

An uneasy silence rested between the three people now standing by the fireplace. They had offered her water, but she had no interest in anything but the boy. He looked well, that was important, but she knew the psychological damage that this couple was capable of. It had been seven days since she had seen him, but it felt much longer than that. She studied his eyes to try and get some understanding of what he might be feeling, but if he was scared, he did not show it. He was too young to really understand what was happening. He had toys and, whatever else they might be, the people holding him here were his family, even if he had only just met them.

"We are glad you are safe. You shouldn't have wandered off like that," her father said in a measured tone.

So, this was how they were going to play it. Give her an opportunity to say it was a mistake, that she was confused. For a moment, she considered playing along. Maybe it would be safer, but as she looked into his blank stare, she could see what it was costing him to offer this.

Years of training had taught her to look behind the words. It might be safer, but it would not help her.

"Why have you brought us here? You had no right."

The man was fourteen years older than the last time she had seen him, but he was no less imposing. He had always been a large man, and decades of manual labour had given him a frame that does not simply fade with age.

"We had every right. You are our daughter. You were led away from us and now we have brought you back. We can overlook your–" he paused and glanced at Ollie "–indiscretions. If you step back onto the right path."

Anger was boiling up and she could feel the fury that she had worked so hard to calm rising inside her.

"No!" She sounded firmer than she felt. "I left because I don't want this, I want another way. I have a family now, away from here. That is where I want to be."

Her father looked like someone who had had a carefully prepared script ripped from them. He had not planned for this. He was a leader here and he was used to getting his own way, especially from people like her. As he grasped fruitlessly for words, her mother, who had been quiet until now, spoke up softly.

"Martha, this is not your choice. The Lord has a plan for you, and you must fulfil that. Your father has told you that you will stay, and you must listen to him."

Where the man had retained his stature, her mother seemed to have disappeared to almost nothing in the years since they had seen each other. Her voice was barely more than a whisper and while her words were painful, there was kindness in her eyes.

"I won't be your prisoner. You can't hold me here. It's not lawful. People will be looking."

Her father had regained his composure. Where before he had been trying hard to appear kind, he was now in full authoritarian mode. "You are not a prisoner. This is your home. We had hoped that you and our grandson would comply willingly, grateful to be back where you belong, but now I see this will not be possible. You require more—" he paused again, searching for the right word, "—instruction."

CHAPTER 11

Rob drove them back to the place where they'd had breakfast. The evening crowd had arrived, and the café now had the ambience of a bustling bistro. Saric had helped the owner select her wine list, which had been a small element of the success of the place. It was predominantly focused on the Bordeaux area, but outside the more traditional regions, and sticking to approachable, classic vintages from the mid-2000s. The owner had made an argument for adding some cheap plonk, even suggesting Australian wine, but Saric had advised strongly against it. "Let the high street chains satisfy the tastes of the ignorant," he had suggested. In the end she was convinced; she made less of a margin on the wine than perhaps she could have done, but she had a clean conscience that her guests were getting value for their money. Saric felt she was providing a valuable public service too.

As their starters arrived, Grace gave her observations.

"The business activity is what Tony described. At least the facts he provided are, not his opinion of how it is being run. Jane's side of the business has been building nicely. Tony's is winding down. It is still profitable overall. They service a wide range of clients with all the usual business affairs. I could find nothing unusual in any of Jane's files or emails. For what it's worth, she looks to have been a good accountant and always tried to do the right thing for her clients. Her phone records show that she would often call clients in the evening. For example, most days after work recently she had been speaking to the treasurer of one of the charities she works with. You saw the office today, the rest of the team are strictly nine to five, so that makes her stand out a bit; she seemed to really care. I looked for any disputes with clients or employees but there wasn't anything out of the ordinary; a few clients asking for money off bills and that sort of thing, but nothing that would indicate anyone was particularly angry with the firm generally, or with Jane in particular. If pressed, I would suggest there are two people who you might want to look into a bit more. I've emailed both of you their details. One of them is an old client who successfully made a claim against the firm for some incorrect advice last year. It wasn't of huge value but some of the emails he sent to Jane were a bit aggressive – there are copies on the file. The other is a manager that Jane fired after he sent some inappropriate texts to one of his team. It seems he thought he was treated unfairly, although looking at the evidence on the file, I'd say he was lucky to get away with just losing his job."

Grace trailed off slightly, which did not go unnoticed by Saric. "What else?" he said with a look of immense interest.

Saric had an ability like no one else Rob had ever met for seeing when there was more to something than met the eye.

"It steps slightly outside my remit and I would be speculating." There was a note of hesitation in Grace's voice but Saric only nodded. "You asked me to look at Jane, and that's what I did, but it seems Jane was looking at Tony."

Saric sat up a little straighter. "What do you mean?"

"Well, the filing system there is set up like many other firms. There is a shared file for each client, which anyone in the business would have access to. They use that to store their clients' records, letters and other notes. But each member of staff also has their own private file that only they can view. In places I've worked at in the past, staff would have used these to store personal files, such as performance reviews and that sort of thing. Work-related items that they wouldn't necessarily want their colleagues to see."

Grace paused slightly, as a small smile flashed across her face. It was a long time since she had worked in a role that required formal performance reviews and even longer since she had taken any notice of what her senior colleagues thought about her.

"Jane's personal files contained all the usual items, but there were also some items relating to Tony; a few emails between him and a client as well as some of the firm's bank records. There was no context to any of it, but it looks to me like Jane was reviewing Tony's work."

"Isn't that normal? One colleague consulting another?" Saric asked.

"It is, but not like this. That might happen if there was a complex question where the answer wasn't clear, but that could be stored in the main shared file. This is different. The emails related to payments being made to the firm and by the firm on behalf of this client. It's very unusual for firms to handle money for their clients, there are lots of reasons why it's risky and there are very strict conditions about when it can happen. It's often an indication of money laundering. Now, I'm not saying that's what's happening here, I don't have any evidence for that, but it is unusual, and I think it would be worth looking into it a little further."

"Tony's emails, who were they from?"

"That's where it gets really interesting." Grace's eyes were shining now. She was enjoying the challenge of this and looked rather happy that she may have beaten Saric to a connection. "They were from a business called JC Motors based in Kent. They were from the owner, a man named Jim."

CHAPTER 12

After dinner, Rob left Saric and Grace and returned to his house. They had been on the go for most of the last forty-eight hours and his first thought was to head straight to bed, but hundreds of restless nights had taught him that sleep would not arrive for some time, so instead he made a pot of tea and settled down in the small living room to gather his thoughts.

Since working with Saric, Rob had barely been at home. The business was thriving and despite Saric's refusal to advertise his services, it was rare that they didn't have an active case requiring their attention. His tiny cottage had once been carefully maintained, but the living room reflected the lack of attention he'd paid to it in recent years. A layer of clutter covered most surfaces and the once tidy bookshelves were overstuffed with books on various subjects. While Rob's usual preference was for non-fiction, there were also copies of many classic works, which he intended to read but somehow never quite got round to picking up.

Rob was seated in a cosy leather armchair in the corner of the room. It had been carefully chosen many years ago, shortly after moving into the cottage, after months of scouring various local antiques shops. Sitting in that chair brought Rob a sense of comfort, which he rarely felt elsewhere these days. Working with Saric had taught him a lot, and one of the things he held onto most tightly was that it was important to evaluate his conclusions independently of his colleague. Saric was incredibly bright, with a lightning-fast mind, but that often brought a level of confidence in his own conclusions that required an alternative perspective. Rob enjoyed this role, partly because of the mental challenge and the potential to have a positive impact on solving cases, but also, and he was less happy to admit this part, because he was at heart incredibly competitive and beating Saric to a connection between facts brought him immense pleasure.

Seemingly minutes later, Rob jolted awake to the sound of his doorbell. He leapt up, thinking that a visitor at this time of night must mean there was news, and then slumped slightly as he realised that light was streaming through the windows.

A glance at his phone showed him that it was 7.30 am, still early for guests but hardly the middle of the night. Drowsily, he found his way to the front door to find Saric standing waiting.

Rob's thoughts often tormented him so that sleep never arrived. As a result, he felt he existed in a state of constant tiredness. By contrast, Saric seemed to barely need any sleep at all.

Seeing Rob's dishevelled appearance seemed to set him back slightly, but nonetheless he continued. "Sorry, it's early, but I thought you would be up by now. I want to make a visit to this Jim. I ran him through Sense Check last night and this guy is not a nice man. In fact, he's the sort of guy that might stretch as far as murder."

"Go on," said Rob, who was developing a strong urge for coffee. He worried for a moment about waking his wife and son, but let it go.

"I have coffee in the car," said Saric, pre-empting Rob's complaint.

"Fine, thanks, fill me in in the car then."

As Saric drove them off, Rob started to wake up with the aid of the bean-to-cup Americano Saric had served him in a flask.

"Last night," explained Saric. "I had a chat with one of my police contacts. The only Jim that seemed likely is a man called James Gallagher. He owns a string of garages around here, including a bunch of hand carwash centres. He pumps them full of Eastern European boys sold a promise – the normal modern slavery story – and moves them on before they get settled. The whole thing is a front for laundering his money. Drug money. He's had a go at everything over the years: pills, acid, coke and always weed. He's not had it all his own way, but he has always managed to come out on top."

"Why don't they just nick him, then?"

"The usual," said Saric. "He has enough police in his pocket to keep ahead of any play, and at the end of the day he's just not that interesting. Someone has to sell the drugs and as long as he's not threatened, he keeps himself pretty much to himself."

"And Tony Spencer is doing his accounts?"

"Seems pretty likely, right?"

"And Grace reckons Jane was onto him?"

"Maybe, yes," said Saric.

"So, you want to do what?"

"Ask him."

"You have something in your back pocket, then?"

"Not really, I'm just going to appeal to his better nature."

"No way," said Rob. "You're going to blag your way into a conversation with the local drug boss and ask him if he killed our client? That's possibly the worst plan you've ever had."

"Well, I have one thing. Umím plynně česky."

"Ha!" laughed Rob. "Got it, so what are you? Concerned brother, prospective supplier, come on, what are you going for?"

"I thought I'd give it a go as a Czech detective looking for lost citizens. If we bump into our favourite goon, it needs to hang together."

"Fine, and what am I?" Rob was smiling.

"My British appointed administrator," said Saric.

Rob laughed out loud. It was ridiculous, but it would be fun to see how far they could get with it. "You could have at least told me before we left," he said, "so I could get tooled up."

"That should be fine. I'm told Jim is not one to make a mess. If he kicks off with us, it won't be until later that we have to worry."

"Oh great," said Rob.

"Look, I need you here," said Saric, taking a more serious tone. "I'm going to ask him about Jane, and you need to tell me what his answer means. So, drink all that coffee and make sure you're paying attention."

"OK, will do," said Rob. This was a lot of effort and risk to give him the opportunity to make an observation; he would make sure it was worth it.

*

James 'Jim' Callagher's head office was at the back of a mechanics yard in an industrial estate ten minutes off the A23. It was nicely spaced out from the other units. Saric drove them into the estate, did not look at the sign and went straight through to the garage site.

"I need to see Jim Callagher," he announced to the man inside the greasy reception area. He laid on the eastern European accent a bit. Saric held out some formal identification, which Rob recognised as his generic formal looking badge. A short period of negotiation took place, where Rob stayed silent, and Saric insisted they would not be leaving before a conversation with Mr Callagher had taken place. Rob, taking his role seriously, was now noticing everything. Saric was psychologically overpowering this man. As Saric spoke, the man's eyes flicked up and to the right, as he searched his imagination for answers he could not find. His pupils were widening, and his breath shortened a little. In the end, the man relented and agreed to take advice from behind the shut door at the back. He emerged with a man who looked in his early sixties. He had worn skin, strong looking hands and alert eyes.

"Who the hell are you, and what do you want?" asked Jim Callagher.

"I am a Czech diplomat. You employ a number of our citizens. I am concerned about their working conditions, but I am not here for that. Today, at least. No, today, I am looking for Johan Brenschek. He wrote to his mother to say he was going to see your accountant to discuss his employment rights. And now your accountant is dead. Murdered. And Johan is missing. And I want to know what you think about this."

Rob absorbed everything he could about Jim Callagher at this moment. He watched his eyes and searched for any small movement in his face. His body language gave nothing away, there was no movement at all. Rob allowed himself to take everything in without noticing anything directly. He let it all flow into his unconscious mind, so the concluding sense could emerge. *Not him*, he thought. *He doesn't know what Saric is talking about.*

"What I think about this," said Jim, "is that I couldn't give two shits who you are, or who you are looking for. You need to piss off, and if I see your face again, we are going to have a problem."

It was a predictable response, but Rob sensed Jim was holding a little back, just in case this odd foreigner was genuinely something to be concerned about.

"Fine," said Saric, "if you are not going to help, I shall find our citizen another way. And if you turn out to be involved, you will have the full force of the Federation Security coming for you, I can assure you of that."

And with that, Saric spun round and paced off.

"Federation Security!" laughed Rob, as they drove out of the estate. "Where the hell did that come from?"

"It just slipped out," said Saric. *Too much Star Trek*, he thought to himself.

CHAPTER 13

Saric dropped Rob at home to get cleaned up. They agreed to meet later for lunch and a chat. He wanted to make some calls, and also connect Sense Check more closely to Jim Callagher. Organised crime was a nuisance. Someone like Jim Callagher did not stay in position without being bright enough to keep his distance from the frontline crime. If he was connected to Jane's murder, there would be layers to unpeel. And the police would be a mixed bag, too; Callagher would be well known to them, but also likely to have a few friendlies in position. Saric sighed when he thought about it. He could just trust Rob's judgment and move on, and maybe he would, but a local crime boss this close to an investigation was hard to ignore. It would take a collection of facts of some substance for Saric to move in a direction away from Rob's assessment, but he would if he had to. Facts never lie.

He spent the next few hours with Sense Check. It was not particularly fruitful. Yes, the system was able to connect, at least in principle, Jim Callagher with various potentially criminal activities. The car wash business was a thin cover for money laundering and people trafficking.

Saric concluded the police could have pulled it down with ease but chose not to. He was not sure what he felt about that morally, so he thought about something else instead. Overall, he did not feel like he had progressed a great deal.

Next were some calls. The police investigation had not moved forward much, but he could not get hold of his best source, Deputy Chief Stephens. Frustrated by an unsatisfactory morning, Saric left his house to meet Rob on the high street.

Lunch was good, but Rob was disappointed to hear that Saric's morning had not advanced the case. Grace's contribution seemed to be pointing them towards Callagher, but they were a long way from connecting him to Jane. The dessert menus ignored, a second bottle of wine was ordered and the afternoon written off by mutual unsaid consent. Before long, the conversation had moved on from the case to a debate over whether it was morally acceptable to drive a classic Ferrari given the state of the environment. Neither of them really cared, so they shifted their positions as soon as they thought they were winning just to drag the discussion out. By the time they left the restaurant, after a brandy each, the conversation had dropped further, as the two of them argued over who, of all their clients, was the best looking. Saric suggested they pop by the wine shop, so they could carry on their chat back at his place.

It went through Rob's mind that he should get home to his wife, and that he would have to hide how drunk he was. His head spun at the thought and he threw up on the pavement.

Saric looked at Rob as if he knew what he was thinking. "Come on, mate," he said, "let's have a drink and talk shit."

Rob agreed. They bought some wine, which Rob double bagged, and they headed to Saric's place.

The town had thinned out by the time they neared the road that Saric's long drive joined. The closest houses to his were far enough away that he did not have to think of them as neighbours, which suited him. The short walk had sobered them both up a little. The discussion had turned to the moral case for vegetarianism, and just as Rob was rehashing a point he had heard on the radio about the devastation of farming soya beans, a hatchback screamed around the corner at the top of the road. It shot down the street towards them and skidded to a stop. Three men jumped out. Rob put his bag of wine down on the floor.

There was no time for discussion. No talking these men down. They had only one thing on their minds. Ten years ago, Rob would have frozen to the spot, like most normal people confronted with violence. The men coming towards them looked like those that lived with brutality as part of their lives; maybe it had always been part of their lives. But now Rob had found the power of operating as if you had nothing to lose. As for Saric, Rob had no idea what was in his life story that gave him the ability to accept confrontation without hesitation or fear. At moments like this, Saric was a destructive man. A dark, lethal force.

"We have a message from Jim Callagher," the first man said without losing pace. He carried a foot-long cosh in his right hand. The second man, at the first's side, was much younger, and he was carrying a baseball bat. The third man, who was slightly behind and between the other two, was the young man from Tony Spencer's office.

Saric and Rob wasted no time in clever retorts. The only thing Rob processed in that instant was to unlock a spiralling, silver tornado within his imagination. This was a technique he had developed over the years as a metaphorical vision for power and speed – the two words that for Rob was what you needed to fight. In principle, it was a simple sub-modality exercise, designed to trigger a profound response in his unconscious, and it was highly effective. In a blink of an eye, Rob's body transformed, as if there was an explosion of energy shooting straight up from the earth below him and into every muscle. He went from the soft physique of a man that had never had to suffer the everyday difficulties of a hard life, to the pumped muscularity of a pissed-off bull.

Next to him, Saric did not seem to change at all, except his eyes, which opened very wide and fixed intently on the man coming towards him. The calm reaction was disturbing to Rob. What had those eyes seen? Rob was glad Saric was on his side.

The cosh was swung, aiming for the left side of Rob's face. He half stepped back onto his right leg, opening his hips and pulling his head back just out of range, but without ducking. His left arm spun round, connecting with the attacker's wrist. Just for a moment, the attacker was off balance, and before he could bring the cosh back around, Rob drove his fist hard into his jaw. There was a loud cracking noise as the jaw broke. The man's eyes flashed wild with pain, rage and, Rob thought, confusion. He did not go down, though. He raised the cosh, looking to bring it straight down on Rob's head this time. It was not a skilful attack, and Rob felt as if the man was operating almost in slow motion. Rob stepped inside the attack, using a head block with his left arm. The cosh missed his head but crashed against his shoulder. Rob felt nothing. He drove up from his legs into an uppercut blow with his elbow. This time, his opponent's jaw was smashed into several pieces, along with a bunch of teeth. The man howled in pain, blood pouring from his mouth as he stumbled back and fell first to his knees, and then face down, as the shock sent him unconscious. Rob's face was covered with splashes of blood, his eyes were wild and his adrenaline was pumping so hard that his whole body shook and bobbed.

He looked over at Saric, who had, it seemed, broken the first man's leg. The young man from the office had stalled with the brutality of the first encounter, looking back at the car as if he wanted something from it. They had misjudged this job, Rob thought. This was supposed to be a beating not a killing, hence bats and coshes rather than guns or knives. The young man had no weapon. Rob guessed he was just here to give the message. Now, though, despite the odds having turned against him, he prepared to take Saric on. He knew no other way. So, fists raised, he circled Saric. Saric gave nothing away and did not even raise his hands above his waist. Saric saw Rob moving to join them.

"We don't need to kill him," Saric warned. He could see Rob was not processing rational thought.

Instinctively, Rob reached down and took a bottle of wine out of its bag, holding it like a weapon. Saric took two steps around the young man, flicking a hand harmlessly up towards his face to engage him. The man turned with him, and Rob smashed the bottle on the back of his head. The young man went down. The bottom of the bottle shot off and caught Saric on the side of his head and ear, leaving a cut. Other shards of glass flew back up into Rob's own face. He felt blood trickle gently down his neck.

"Subtle," said Saric.

"Sorry." Rob looked genuinely upset.

"Don't worry, mate, I knew what you were doing. It seemed like a good idea at the time. One thing, though. Please tell me that was not the ninety-eight Saint-Emilion Grand Crus."

Rob looked at what was left of the bottle in his hand. "Oh dear," he said, and now Saric looked genuinely upset.

Saric made a call. He said something to the person on the line about clearing up a mess, announced to Rob that it would be sorted, and the two of them left the scene to clean themselves up and drink the remaining inferior wine. Rob felt pretty sure Saric might allow them to dip into his wine cellar on a night like this, so they would manage just fine.

CHAPTER 14

JANUARY 2016

As a girl, Martha had been exposed to what she now knew was a relentless program of mind control, involving endless repetition of mindless tasks, ritual, prayers and chants learned by rote. Every sense was filled. Everywhere you looked were images of the faith. When she hugged her mum as a child, she could feel the sharp edges of the crucified Christ pushing into her. Church services were filled with incense. She had come to love the smell. Questioning was pointless, as the answer to all things was made by reference to the Great Lord's will, which was either lifted straight from the Bible or some other text adopted as a supplement to the truth. Or it was interpreted by an elder whose knowledge was itself an authority. And everyone did what they were told.

Only when the woman who went on to free her showed her a different way to think did she realise that independent thought had value. It was like a great tidal wave smashing away all that she thought was real. You must question what you are told, she learned. It was profound, and absolutely devastating to her state of mind. But with patient teaching, she came to know how to think for herself, and how to defend herself from doubt.

At first, she wanted with all her heart to reject what was being shown to her. It was not safe, or comfortable. It was easier to retreat to certainty and block out all doubt. It was easier to fill her heart with the love of the Great Lord and let the rest of the world simply drift away. But doubt had got into her, and it would not let her go.

She had not escaped from the community so much as she had been escaped. It was not her action but the action of others that had freed her. On her own, she would not have had enough courage to do it.

In the years after, once in the UK and no longer Martha, she dedicated herself to a study of the mind. In part it was to protect herself from the residual damage of her upbringing, the bit of her that was still capable of longing for certainty, and in part it was with a resolute determination to help others also trapped in their own corrupted mindsets. She accumulated letters after her name, ultimately becoming both a neuroscientist and a cognitive therapist.

She had not built her new life on her own. Despite her upbringing, she believed in true love, and that she had found it. She saw her son as an expression of that love. So, she had to fight. Fight not to let them into her mind. Fight to get her son back home. Fight to prove them all wrong.

It was not a plan, though. She resisted everything they tried and got the sense they were starting to give up on her. She was getting more time to think. She could feel some clarity trying to break through in her mind.

There was a small, hesitant knock at the door, which opened to reveal a round-faced man, perhaps a few years younger than she was.

"Hello Martha, my name is Daniel."

She still drew back at the sound of a name that had not been hers for such a long time.

"I will be supervising your continued reintroduction to the Community. When the appropriate time has passed and you have relinquished your present ways, it has been decided that you will become my wife."

She stood in stunned silence. Explanations of how she was already married caught in her throat, as she thought of her husband and what he must be feeling. He would be searching for her, she could not let herself doubt that, but she had kept this life tightly shut away, even from him. How would he ever find her when she was hundreds of miles from home?

She could not express any of this to the stranger standing across from her, who'd been sent to her by her parents from what seemed like another life and which had now crashed into reality.

For his part, the young man looked at her with the absolute confidence that young men in this community were brought up to have. Certain of his place in this tiny, isolated world. Never questioning why it was like this.

He looked young and, perhaps, under all that, a little uneasy about what was now being asked of him.

CHAPTER 15

The encounter with Jim's men, followed by too much wine with Saric, meant that Rob fell unconscious as soon as he lay down in bed that night. When he woke the next morning, he felt as if a great weight was lying across his left shoulder. It took a few moments for his mind to catch up with his body and remember the fight. He tentatively moved his arm; it was stiff but not seriously injured. He stood under a scalding hot shower for as long as he could bear and then carefully got dressed, whilst nursing his arm. His shoulder was puffy where he had taken the blow, and there were several small cuts across his right cheek. He was pretty sure they had picked all the glass out the night before.

He felt his way downstairs, bleary eyed and craving caffeine, to find Saric sitting at the dining table, two mugs of coffee placed carefully on coasters in front of him. He had never given Saric a key to the cottage, but that didn't stop his friend from letting himself in whenever it was convenient to him. At first, Rob found this intrusive, but as the years had passed, he had learned to enjoy the familiarity between them, although he never had worked out how Saric got in.

"Morning," he said, not yet able to engage in full conversation. He grabbed the mug eagerly and took a long gulp. The liquid burned his throat, but the warmth helped immediately.

"I've had Phillip on the phone already this morning wanting an update. I've told him what we have but he is pushing for more. I wanted to run a few ideas past you."

Rob had also learned to accept that Saric didn't always observe social niceties, but he concluded that he would take a friend who brought good coffee over one who feigned interest in how he was any time.

Rob glanced at the front of his phone. "It's only ten past eight, he's keen."

"He's worried the police are after him. I would be too if I were him. I told him that."

Before Saric could update Rob, they were interrupted by the buzzing of his phone. It was Grace and, even though her voice was muffled as Saric held the phone to his ear, Rob could tell that she was agitated. Saric said very little but listened closely to what she was saying.

"Yes, we will come straight away. We will be there in no more than an hour."

He hung up the phone and clicked through a few screens, as if he had either forgotten Rob was there or had not considered that he might also want to know who had just called. This was one of Saric's more annoying traits. He had an ability to absolutely prioritise whatever action he thought was most important at a particular time. This focus made him an excellent investigator but was infuriating when Rob was worried about their friend and what she might have said to him.

Eventually, when Saric had satisfied himself with whatever was on his phone, he looked back up at Rob. "Grace has another idea. She thinks we are on the wrong track with Jim."

"Yes, we've just agreed he doesn't fit the profile, but what did she say?" Rob was impatient now.

"We're going to meet her now so she can show us. She says it will be easier to explain that way."

Both men were subdued on the journey to town. The usual comfortable silence was heavy with exhaustion. The adrenaline that had carried them through their somewhat tense interview with Jim and the subsequent encounter with his men had drained them both and would take a while to replace. They travelled in the kind of weary silence that arises not when people are busy with their own thoughts, but when they are simply too exhausted to think at all. Rob's shoulder was now throbbing.

The roads were clear, which gave them time to stop for breakfast and still arrive at Grace's at the time Saric had suggested. Saric just about tolerated the Americano that was served to them in the service station coffee shop, but he could not resist commenting on how it did not live up to the dark roasted, single origin Costa Rican coffee he now preferred, after having completed an exhaustive search of online coffee bean dealers. The shop was a small branch of a large chain and Rob thought the coffee was perfectly acceptable, and it also helped him to swallow the painkillers he'd bought in the newsagent next door. However, he chose not to argue the point with Saric, who was taking out his frustration at the case – and their morning – on the plastic lid, which he removed from the paper cup with a look of absolute distaste.

Grace's office was on the top floor of a converted town house in one of the town's better areas. The complex and highly confidential nature of what she did meant that she did not work for one of the big consultancy firms, with their large glass-fronted offices in the big cities, but instead employed a small but highly competent team that operated from a much more discrete location. As Saric and Rob stepped through the door and into a spacious, elegantly furnished open plan area, which seemed to function as a reception and informal meeting area, several heads turned and hesitated just longer than was necessary to take in the new arrivals.

While the dress code in the office might be described as business casual, Rob could see that many of Grace's employees spent more on one haircut than he had on his whole outfit today, and of course, this was not helped by the prominent cuts on his face and the bruises on his knuckles. Saric was unaware of the looks they were receiving, possibly because they were not aimed at him. He had an incredible ability to blend in wherever he went, and he strode confidently ahead of Rob before knocking on one of the doors that led off the central area.

Grace had a spacious office in the corner of the building, with wide views across the park and towards a large lake. She was sitting behind an oversized desk that made her appear even smaller than usual, and the morning sun that poured in through the floor-to-ceiling windows illuminated her face.

As she saw Rob and Saric, a wide smile grew across her face; she was about to greet them when she noticed Rob's face. "What happened?" she gasped, pushing her chair away from her desk and hurrying over to them, without even taking the time to step back into the pair of heels that she looked to have kicked off under the desk before they arrived. She stepped closer and inspected their injuries. "Did Jim Callagher do this to you?" she asked, with a determination on her face that suggested that if he had, she would go and do the same to him.

"Not directly, but his men did. Overall, I think they came off worse," said Rob.

As Saric did nothing to reassure Grace, Rob added, "We are both fine, though, it looks worse than it is, and they definitely got the message that violence is not the right way to approach this."

"Can I get you anything?" Grace asked with deep concern. Rob realised that she would be thinking that she had signposted them to Jim and that she would only feel worse when she found out their visit had been for nothing. Knowing that Saric might not approach this discussion with the sensitivity it required, he gently declined her offer and guided her back to the desk, as he talked her through their encounter with Jim.

While he certainly did not feel the need to shield her from the truth, he may have left out some of the finer points of their encounter with the men.

"But I understand from Saric that you have another idea." He moved the subject on gently, trying to steer Grace away from any role she might have felt she had in the previous evening's events.

"Well, yes, but if Jim is worried enough to send those men after you, isn't he your main suspect?"

"Maybe," Saric agreed, "but I'd like to keep an open mind at this stage. Sense Check is indicating too many uncertainties to really be sure, so let's see what else we can find."

"Something has been bothering me ever since we left the office last night, but it wasn't until I got the chance to look at the data this morning that I worked out what it was. It might be nothing, and he certainly doesn't seem like the right type of person, but I've seen it now, so I think you need to see it."

Grace hit a few keys on her laptop and a large screen on the wall to her left lit up. It showed some sort of database output containing times and dates and what seemed to be descriptions of tasks performed. Jane's name featured many times on this list, along with three other names that Rob did not recognise. With a few more taps on the keyboard a second screen lit up, this one showing a long list of phone calls and emails.

Grace stood up to move closer to the screens, her impressive heels now back on, as if to demonstrate that she was back in fully professional mode. Rob turned his chair to face them. Saric's eyes never left Grace.

"You remember yesterday, when I told you how accountancy firms work? It's basically a case of put hours on the clock and bill them. Each employee completes a timesheet that records what they do with every minute of every day. This then becomes the central record of all the time spent, which is used as the basis to charge fees."

Grace pointed to the first screen, with the database shots. "This is the time record for one of Jane's clients. I'm using it as an indication of how it would normally work before I show you the interesting part. You can see from the phone and email records that over the last month, Jane made three calls and sent six emails to this client. When you look at the timesheet, you can see entries corresponding to each of these interactions on the relevant days. Some of it is from Jane and some of it is from members of her team, who would have been helping her, but the point is that the times and dates correspond exactly with the evidence.

"Jane has fifty-six clients at the firm. Obviously, I haven't yet checked all of them. In fact, I was hoping that might be something that your software could help me with." She glanced at Saric, who nodded in agreement. A slight smile crossed his face, in equal measure pride in his work and appreciation that Grace had noticed it. "For the ones I have checked, all the records correspond exactly, which is what I would expect from someone who has been repeatedly described to us as a person who likes to follow rules. That's true for all the records I have checked, except one."

Grace swiped the screens and new data, in the same format as before, populated them. It was for a client called South Downs Theatre. On the left was a short list of timesheet entries, this time for Jane and one other employee, while on the right was a long list of calls and emails. Rob noticed that this was primarily calls, with only a few emails, which were all sent much earlier in the month.

"This is the record for one of Jane's charity clients. It's a small organisation that puts on amateur productions over towards Crawley."

Rob thought that using the South Downs description to refer to an organisation based in one of the less beautiful towns in the region was bold, but he didn't comment.

"As you can see, Jane was making and receiving lots of calls with the treasurer, but very few of these were recorded on her timesheet."

"It looks like a lot of the calls were made out of hours," Rob said. "Is it possible that she was just helping out the charity in her spare time? Perhaps they are friends and the calls are not work related." Rob found it hard to believe that a small provincial charity could be connected with a murder, and while he did not want to dismiss Grace's suggestion out of hand, he was keen to get back to the question of how to deal with Jim.

"It is possible, but around forty per cent of Jane's business was with charities, so I'm not sure why she would offer free advice to this one in particular. And the fact that the calls were made in the evening wouldn't matter. From the review of the other clients, I can see that she charged for lots of out-of-hours calls to them. That would be usual practice anyway – accountants like to get paid.

"I agree that they could be friends, but there are often three or four calls a day and some of them last late into the night. I don't know how often you speak to your friends, but to me that seems like a lot. Look, , it might be nothing, but look at the calls. There are increasing numbers every day right up until the day before Jane was killed, and then nothing. If this was an urgent matter, wouldn't the treasurer have tried to get hold of her since then?"

Rob had to agree that this was a good point, and the fact that Saric was sitting silently and completely still meant he also agreed that the idea was worth pursuing, his mind having moved on to consider some other element of the puzzle that would no doubt become clear given time.

"Do we know anything more about the treasurer?" Rob asked.

"All I have is the email records, which show his name is Colin Edwards. As well as being the treasurer of the charity, he is the financial controller of a small manufacturing firm on that big business park on the edge of Crawley. I know that because he sometimes emailed Jane from his work email address. I've printed off all the correspondence that is on the file for you, so his details are in there. There is also an administrative assistant who deals with the day-to-day running of the charity's finances. Her details are in the file too."

She handed Rob a thin file that showed her company's logo on the front. While he had known since they first met that Grace had all the attributes to carve out a great career, Rob had only just come to appreciate how successful she really was, and he reflected on how fortunate they were to have her involved in the case.

Along with the paper copies, Grace sent the electronic file to Saric, who set Sense Check the task of cross referencing the information they contained against its other sources. After a short time, it fed back its results, which corroborated Grace's work and demonstrated that the way time had been charged to the theatre was not consistent with Jane's other clients.

Sense Check also showed that South Downs Theatre was in financial trouble, which was not unlike many other comparable organisations in its reference population. Colin Edwards was registered as a trustee of the charity and had been for the last three years. Beyond that, Sense Check found very little on him, other than a small piece from the website of a local paper dated two Christmases ago, in which he was featured in a photo of the cast of a pantomime. One of Sense Check's limitations was that it was only able to draw conclusions based on the information presented to it. In some cases, where the individual was quite well known, there might be quite a lot of publicly available sources, but with others, where people led smaller, less public lives, there was much less that Sense Check could do to help.

Despite their conclusion that Tony and Jim were unlikely to be involved, pursuing this new angle of investigation felt like a waste of time to Rob, and he was surprised when Saric agreed that they should look into Colin Edwards' background. Rob could not help but feel that if the suggestion had come from anyone else but Grace, Saric might have been much harder to convince that this was a worthy angle. Rob wasn't sure why this bothered him so much. Grace was a remarkable woman and he was confident she would not have suggested this man as a possibility unless she had good reason to do so.

Rob called Colin Edwards using the number listed on the theatre group's website and asked if they could meet. Colin was aware of Jane's death; Tony had called him a few days earlier, but he seemed more concerned that his affairs had been reassigned to a newly qualified accountant and that Tony had not taken over himself. Rob did not like to form views of people over the phone, there was too much that could be missed when you could not look someone in the eye and see how they moved, but from this limited interaction, Colin seemed to be exactly what the background profile said he would be; a mild-mannered man heading towards retirement. A little socially awkward, perhaps, but nothing more.

Colin said he was very happy to meet them, but he explained that he was tied up in final rehearsals for his latest production and would not be able to see them until after the next day's matinee.

CHAPTER 16

As the performance did not start until 2.30 pm, Rob had the next morning to himself. The exact nature of his partnership with Saric had never really been formalised. They had met around five years ago and, while working closely together on a case, Saric had engaged Rob in a role that could perhaps be best described as a consultant. Initially, this had been on an ad hoc basis, whenever a case required some of Rob's time, but gradually this increased until two years ago, when Rob had taken a sabbatical from his job as a teacher at a well-respected local private school to consult on a more regular basis. Strictly speaking, he was still on that sabbatical. He was keeping his options open, he told the few colleagues who still bothered to ask him about it, although privately he knew that he had no intention of returning.

When there was nothing to do on a case, Rob's time was his own. Instinctively, he walked towards the corner of the living room where his weights were kept. Training was part of his routine and the events of the last few days had inspired him to work even harder. While violence was not common in the cases he and Saric worked on, they did seem to encounter more trouble than most, and they couldn't always rely on their adversaries being quite so underprepared as the men they had fought had been.

Before he even reached the makeshift gym, he realised that, while his mind was definitely ready to enhance his skills, his body was in no state to do so. He looked around the room seeking some other way to pass the hours until he could meet Saric, aware that he should feel pleased to have a morning off to relax and rest.

Looking guiltily at the clutter that hung around the room, he reached aimlessly for the first book that came to hand and sat down to read. His eyes scanned the text and his hands turned the pages, but he could not focus on the words in front of him. The silence that hung in the room was suffocating. It was like all the air had been sucked from it, and he was suddenly aware of the emptiness around him. He switched on the radio and flicked through the stations, hoping that some music might turn down the churning of his mind. Nothing felt right. One song, a new release from an artist he was vaguely aware of, was too upbeat, the next, from an old hits station, was too slow. He avoided anything where he could hear people speaking, unable to give his attention to other people this morning. Accepting that no song would be right, he left the radio humming unsatisfactorily in the background and went back to his book.

Focus.

If he could just get through one page without letting his mind wander.

The old house creaked as the boiler fired up and started to heat the water tank. He knew he was alone, and he was familiar with the sounds of the house, but for one fraction of a second he could not help but wonder who was moving around to make that noise. Did they need him?

Back to the book.

But it was no good. He placed the book on top of a precarious pile of other works that he had tried and failed to read.

What else could he do? He sat in the small patch of sun that had found its way through the window and into the tired room. He was tired too. He had thought about moving many times, to somewhere that did not hold so many memories; a place where he could switch off the part of his mind that would not let go. He would not forget but perhaps somewhere new he would be able to close it off. But not feeling this would be worse than feeling it. It would be like some additional act of betrayal.

So, he sat there, counting seconds and minutes, breathing in and breathing out, marking time until the next thing happened, where he could step outside this creaking cottage full of memories and try to make things right again.

CHAPTER 17

MARCH 2016

It had been some months since the young man, Daniel, had been introduced to the situation. He was meant to control her reintroduction, which the Elders were forced to accept was more difficult than they had anticipated. Daniel had patiently explained how he would allow her to recognise her love for him. The Great Lord had brought her to him. The Great Lord's love would flow through her, and into him. It was inevitable.

Martha disagreed. Initially, she had focused only on getting out. She had tried and failed. She had fought them since, worried that if she gave them any ground, she might not be strong enough to keep them out of her mind. She remained resolute that she would escape and take her son back home, but she had come to realise she would need some help. This was going to be a slower process than she wanted, but she would get it done.

Her plan had formed. There was no physical threat, they were not after that yet. First, they wanted to get inside her head. Knowing she would be exposed to these people for a period of time, she would take steps to prepare herself in the defence of her mind.

Then, once confident in allowing herself to hear what they said instead of rejecting everything out of hand, she would present them with the Martha they had always wanted.

And lastly, she would take control.

To ready her mind, she spent some time initially investigating the feeling of conflict with what she was being told to believe. She sat on the floor, legs crossed, and pushed that feeling all around her body, as if it were entering every cell. When she felt confident that she had captured that feeling, she switched focus to finding the key words that would protect her from enabling them to get inside her head and rekindle that easy, soft sense of calm that she knew could follow devotion. 'Self' and 'truth' were her watch words. She smiled to herself, as the word truth emerged. Was it not exactly that idea of a truth that sat at the centre of what she had needed to unlearn all those years ago? Despite that, the only word that worked here for her was truth. She thought on it long and hard, worried that maybe the word truth had come to her because she was back with the people who claimed they knew it, and maybe they were already inside her mind. But it was not that. The 'truth' that had emerged as her key word here was bigger and more profound than any religion could handle. It was the idea of a truth not known. The idea that there is a truth out there, but that we humans are simply not built to recognise it, or even really comprehend what it could possibly mean. The notion that the latest species of ape that has existed for a few hundred thousand years on this insignificant planet, designed like all animals to eat, sleep and reproduce, could have evolved to understand the true nature of all things was laughable. There is a truth, but we do not – and never will – know it.

Self was her other key word. That was more obvious to her, and it was one of the first feelings she had become aware of, even when wrapped up in rage and hurt and fear. She was a unique person. Everyone was. She was responsible for her own behaviour, her own thoughts, her own values and beliefs, and even her own sense of identity. This simple recognition was a vital missing part of many of her patients' mental awareness. She must continue to be herself, and to be held accountable for her every thought and action.

Settled on these two key words, she built them out using a simple sub-modalities method neatly described by practitioners of neurolinguistic programming, of which she was one, amongst the myriad other qualifications she had in this field. If 'self' had a colour, what colour would it be? Green. What sort of green? A dark forest green. If you wanted to feel a stronger sense of 'self', would you make the green darker or lighter, or keep it the same? Darker. Do that now . . . and so on, until you have the exact colour to trigger a deep and profound sense of self. Repeat with 'truth', only this time with a shape. It's a sphere; it gets stronger as it gets bigger, and stronger when it rotates, which way? Clockwise. The faster it rotates the stronger it gets.

Finally, she combined the colour of self with the shape of truth, allowing the image to hover in front of her, at chest height. When she knew that the spinning, enlarged, dark green sphere of self and truth was at its most powerful (imagine what it would do to become twice as powerful again . . .) she brought it into herself, allowing that feeling to fill her entire body and mind. She felt completely untouchable. She made no attempt to put the feeling into words, but she knew that as long as she held onto it, they would not get to her.

Not this time.

CHAPTER 18

Rob and Saric arrived early at the theatre, having agreed to watch the show before meeting Colin. Rob had worked hard to persuade Saric that this was a good use of his time.

"Watching a terrible amateur production of some second-rate play won't tell us who killed Jane," Saric had complained.

"Perhaps not," Rob had argued, "but we might get a feel for what kind of man we are dealing with."

The theatre would once have been quite grand, but it had the feeling of a building that had not been looked after for some time. They recognised Colin from his photo in the local paper. He was selling tickets at a small table in front of the box office. Rob and Saric joined a short queue and waited while two groups in front of them bought tickets. Both parties were talking about family members who were appearing in the production. Some of them were excited to spot their loved one but most seemed to be there out of a sense of duty.

When they reached the front of the queue, Colin welcomed them.

They had decided not to introduce themselves at this stage but instead to use the opportunity to learn a bit more about the man.

"We'd like two tickets, please," Rob smiled at Colin.

"Of course, have a look at the plan and let me know where you would like to sit."

While Saric made a show of choosing seats from a half-empty floor plan, Rob had the opportunity to find out more about Colin. Aware that they would soon have to introduce themselves, and not wanting Colin to think they had fooled him, Rob kept the questions light.

"We haven't come across this group before, do you put on many performances?"

"We aim for two shows a year, which usually run for a week each. Then there is the panto, of course, that's the big one. This might be our only show this year, though, funding is difficult to come by, you know." He looked at the two men expectantly.

Rob ignored the plea and pressed on. "Has this production been a success?"

Colin took a deep breath. "Ticket sales are good so far," he said, but he sounded unconvinced and Rob wondered what colour Sense Check would turn that statement when they ran the recording they were currently making through the software back in the office.

"There are some great actors involved and we are very lucky to have a new director who has just moved to the area having retired from London. But the star of the show has to be the mother, I think, you will find her performance incredibly moving."

Rob paid for the tickets and spent the next two hours wishing that he had not pressed Saric so hard to attend the performance. Their brief conversation with Colin had not really told him anything new and the play was so bad that he had to stop himself leaving during the interval. Saric did not appear to notice the overacting or the three separate times the lead character forgot his lines. Saric's mind was elsewhere, working on new theories and processing the information they had already gathered. In Rob's opinion, the new director had made some terrible choices in the staging and was trying to be edgy and bold when he had clearly overestimated the skills of the performers. The mother character, who Colin had identified as being the star of the show, was a slender, rather grey woman who was probably in her mid-forties but looked like she could have been at least ten years older. She was capable enough and did stand out in a pool of performers that lacked any discernible talent, but there was something in her eyes that made Rob uncomfortable. The character was supposed to be a jovial maternal figure, but she looked terrified, as if someone might emerge from the audience at any point and rip her from the stage.

As the performers took their final bow, Saric emerged from his thoughts and Colin strode confidently onto the stage. He made a short speech thanking various patrons and asking for donations. The way he held himself, delivering carefully prepared lines begging the audience for funds as if he was reciting one of the great Shakespeare monologues, made Rob wonder if he did not harbour his own ambition to tread the boards instead of selling tickets in the foyer.

They had arranged to meet Colin in the theatre bar after the performance and headed straight there, managing to grab one of the few tables that were scattered around the room.

The bar filled up quickly. Rob and Saric took a seat in the corner and people watched whilst they waited. All the usual bar behaviours were in evidence; men jostling for position and then waving their arms around in victory as they got served first, passing cheap wine and flat lager around to friends and family. Tubby middle-aged women talking about their kids, or other mums that were not present. Teenage children unsure who to talk to and wishing they were anywhere else.

After a while, members of the cast started to drift out and join their friends and family. This was the opening show of a nine-performance run, and the cast soaked up the reassurances from their loved ones of a job well done. Rob wondered how long the cast members remained 'in character' before returning to their normal family position. However long that feeling lasted, the looks on their faces let Rob know this was a high that, at least for them, was worth all the effort.

Then Colin appeared. He was still wearing his dark blue waistcoat, which must have required a deep breath to do the buttons up. He saw Rob and Saric in the corner and headed their way. As he passed through the crowd, the cast acknowledged him with smiles and some thanks. The other guests did not seem to notice him, which made no impact on his sense of self-importance at all. They were simply ignorant of how the whole show was his doing.

"Hello," he almost shouted, "you must be the private detectives. I should have realised when you bought your tickets, but I wasn't expecting you to watch the performance."

He took a seat. Saric flicked his recording device on and hoped there was not too much background noise. He would load it into Sense Check later.

"Thank you for agreeing to meet us today," said Rob, "and congratulations on the performance."

"Why thank you," said Colin, "wasn't it wonderful? It's a fantastic play as long as you get the right people in the right roles; and we certainly did that." Colin was glowing with pride.

Actually, the whole thing was pretty excruciating, thought Rob, but he just smiled and wondered for a moment why Colin did not trim his nose hairs.

"As I said on the phone, we have been employed by Jane Evans's husband to investigate her recent death. We are meeting as many of her clients as possible to get a full understanding of her circle of contacts and interests. We understand that you are treasurer for this theatre group, and a client of Spencer and Evans. Did you have much to do with

Mrs Evans recently?"

"Well," said Colin, "there is always something when it comes to running a charity. Especially when you have a performance to put on. You know, accounting underpins the success of any venture in the end. It doesn't matter how many supposed great ideas people have, if the numbers don't add up it's not going to get you anywhere. And it's much more complicated than most people think. There's a whole set of special accounting rules, regulatory requirements, documentation, and so on, that comes with running a charity. It is important to keep your accountant up to speed on what you are doing so you don't have to spend ages explaining things later in the year. So, yes, I spoke to her quite often; to help her really."

"I see," said Saric, who did not see, and realised they should have asked Grace along.

"Did you and Jane get on well?" asked Rob.

"I thought she was perfectly competent. But I was just another client to her, I suppose."

"When did you last see her?"

"A couple of weeks ago. I popped into the office to discuss a regulatory point."

"What regulatory point?" asked Saric.

"Do you really want to discuss charity regulation?"

"Yes, please," said Saric.

"All right. Last year, we put some capital into a social investment fund. We negotiated a partial way out of it to realise some cash, and I needed to agree the split between income and capital."

Saric did not have any idea what Colin was talking about, but if it sounded helpful, he thought he could maybe ask Grace to take a look at the transcript.

"I see," said Saric again.

"What time of day did you see her?" asked Rob.

"After work."

"Did you go straight to her office?"

"Yes."

"Was she expecting you?"

"Yes, of course."

"Did she ask to speak to you in person about it, or did you ask to see her?"

"I asked to see her. Look, this really is not very exciting. I called her and said I needed to talk something through with her, and so I popped round a couple of days later to do just that."

"And you resolved the matter?"

"Yes, we reached a sensible agreement."

"And did you speak to her again after that meeting?"

Rob had been watching Colin's eyes closely. He was always reticent to place too much emphasis on eye accessing cues; too often he had drawn a conclusion, only to realise later the subject was reverse oriented, or that he had just tracked the eyes incorrectly. One thing Rob was sure of here; Colin's eyes were moving a lot. His mind was very active.

"No, that was it," said Colin.

"And what were you doing on the 16th June?"

"I went to the theatre. In London, where I used to work. They are showing *The Full Moon* at the moment. It's not bad. I went up on the train from Crawley to Victoria, and I jumped on the tube to Piccadilly Circus, walked to the show, watched it and came home the same way."

Too much detail, thought Rob. "You really like theatre, then?" he asked, without really knowing why.

Colin leaned forward. "The theatre is the greatest of the arts. It's real people bringing words on a page from the imagination of the playwright to life. It's tangible and unreal at the same time. It matters."

Saric was not interested in a discussion about the arts. "Did you think Mrs Evans was acting in any way odd the last time you spoke to her?"

"No, she seemed fine to me. I think she was a little worried that we would not agree on the accounting point, but she got it after I had properly explained it, and the next time we spoke she was fine."

"Would you say the issue you were dealing with was particularly extraordinary for Mrs Evans?" asked Saric.

"I imagine she had to deal with these sorts of things all the time. That's what she was there for at the end of the day."

Saric exchanged a look with Rob. They were both finding this man uninteresting. But they were spared any further conversation, as Colin leaped up without warning.

"I hope that was helpful to you," he said, "I have to join my team now." He lingered for the briefest moment to confirm they were not about to challenge his exit and then bounded off.

The lead actress had entered the bar. Colin tried not to race too fast over to her. When he did reach her, they both seemed unsure what the right greeting was. It ended in a half-aborted hug, which made Rob wince. Colin waved at the barman, with whom he must have made an earlier arrangement. The barman spun round, popped a bottle of champagne and gestured to the customers at the bar to let Colin reach through and collect it, along with two glasses. Saric caught the name on the bottle but could not identify the champagne. *Almost certainly dreadful*, he thought.

Colin poured two glasses and wondered what to do with the bottle he was now clutching.

"You were marvellous," he beamed, "here, a little celebration," and he handed her a glass. She accepted it, but rather than take a sip she stared down at the rim, as if unsure what she had in her hand.

"Thank you," she said, her voice quiet and measured. She looked out of place, like someone had plucked her out of her real life and she had just woken up here in this bar, unsure of how she had got here or what she should do next. She looked around nervously, as if checking who was watching.

"I probably shouldn't have any, though."

Colin's face fell, his gesture had fallen flat.

"It's a lovely thought, it's just, well, it would be difficult to explain."

The look that flashed across Colin's face was difficult to describe. A hint of anger at first – for the smallest fraction of a second – and then, Rob was not sure, maybe disappointment but closer to resignation. As if whatever was unsaid at this moment made him want to react violently and also to pull away. Rob was no stranger to this kind of emotional conflict, having felt this way many times over the last few years when there was no target for the anger that boiled within him. What made

Rob curious was why Colin was displaying these emotions.

"Can I get you something else?" Colin asked.

"An orange juice, please."

While Colin stood at the bar trying desperately to get the attention of the elderly and incredibly slow barman among a crowd of other patrons, the woman he had been speaking to stood silently at the edge of the room. Other cast members entered, glanced around and walked quickly to large groups of friends and family members, as if they did not notice her. Some made an awkward nod in her direction, acknowledging that she was alone, but no one stopped to chat. Sarah did not seem to notice; she simply stood waiting patiently, never once lifting her eyes from the patterned carpet. Her mousy, greying hair fell loosely at her shoulders, her black, knee-length dress was embellished with black sequins and her black heels looked to be slightly too big. Coupled with the inexpertly applied make up, which made her otherwise plain face look garish, and she looked to Rob like a child who had been left alone in her mother's wardrobe at dressing-up time.

She was a slight woman who appeared to make every effort to make herself smaller by drawing in on herself, rounding her shoulders and keeping her head down, as she fidgeted, balancing nervously on the side of the sole of her shoe.

"Here you are." Colin passed her a tall glass. Rob noticed he held onto it for half a second too long as she took it from him.

"It's as if he thinks she owes him," Rob mumbled to Saric, who was staring intently at his phone screen and so gave no response.

The bar was busy and Rob strained to hear the conversation, but he was interested now, not in Colin, who he still thought to be a bore, but in this strange, contradictory woman, who managed to simultaneously look as if she would rather be anywhere else in the world and that there was nowhere else she would rather be.

"I can't stay long, I must get home soon," she was saying.

Colin nodded. "Yes, of course, but just stay for five more minutes and enjoy this, it's all for you."

Colin was standing just a little too close, his elbow resting on the small shelf that ran around the edge of the room, expanding his already wide frame and straining his already tight waistcoat to the point where Rob was concerned that it might burst. He looked proud, as if the entire evening was his doing, as he gestured towards the people standing in the bar. The crowd was already dwindling, as people finished their obligatory post-show drink with their loved ones and made polite excuses for early exits.

Sarah scanned the room, a hint of a smile on her face. "We did well, didn't we?"

"Yes, I think it was worth it."

Rob reflected for a moment on how small some people's lives were. He was in awe of those who found this enough, who could pass their lives through an endless series of amateur plays, evenings in front of the television and trips to the shops at the weekend, without needing to ask why any of it mattered or what else there was to be found from life. If this had once satisfied Rob, it no longer did; there were greater truths to be found and held onto, questions to be asked and answered, and places to be. Even so, he found himself a little envious of this awkward, round man, as he stood proudly next to this nervous grey woman. There was something else, though, a sense that he could not quite put into words, and which made him anxious.

"Shall we go, then? I'd like to get this data into Sense Check and the remote upload function isn't working. The theatre Wi-Fi is awful." Saric's voice interrupted Rob's musings, as he stood up from behind the tiny table. He felt like he had almost grasped something, but it had disappeared as quickly as it arrived.

"I'll see you back at the office, I'm going to stay here a bit longer."

"OK." Saric tried to keep the note of concern out of his voice. He was not completely sure he succeeded. "What are you going to do?"

"I'm sure it's nothing, but there's something not right about those two." He gestured towards Colin and Sarah. Colin was now leaning into Sarah and speaking directly into her left ear, his right hand hovering at her waist. "I'm just going to make sure she gets away safely."

"Fine, but remember, Rob, it's not your job to save everyone."

Saric made his way back to the theatre foyer. As he moved, people instinctively got out of his way. It's usually best to do that when a lump of solid rock animated into human form is walking towards you, even when that person is simply leaving a bar.

Rob sat silently and contemplated drinking another beer while he waited for whatever was playing out in front of him to resolve itself. He fought to resist that temptation; he had a rule against drinking alone, and sometimes he was strong enough to keep to it.

CHAPTER 19

Something about the interaction between Colin and Sarah had made Rob feel uneasy. She was glowing from the success of the play and from Colin's praise of her, but that scared look in her eye was even more obvious now that she was not putting on a show.

If he had doubts about Colin's link to the Jane situation, then he was even less sure about how Sarah might fit in, but Rob was concerned for her and resolved to dig a little further. Even if this had nothing to do with Jane Evans, the idea of a woman being so terrified made his stomach turn.

Before working with Saric, Rob had always imagined that following a suspect would require highly skilled techniques to avoid detection, but having decided that he would like to know more about Sarah, and concluding he had no legitimate reason to ask any further questions, he simply followed her as she left the theatre. In Rob's experience, most people were far too involved in their own preoccupations to pay any attention to what was going on around them, and so he simply got onto the same bus as Sarah and took a seat a few rows behind her. As the bus travelled out of town, towards the residential area, the traffic got lighter and the busy vehicle emptied, as shoppers and commuters reached their stops. Thankfully, Sarah's stop was fairly busy, and Rob was able to let four people get off after her, before disembarking himself.

They were by a small parade of shops, including a convenience store, a hairdressers and a Chinese takeaway. While Rob had not been to this part of town before, it looked much like several other neighbourhoods that had been built in the post-war construction boom. They were just close enough to London to be a viable, if painful, commute, but far enough to benefit from lower property prices and more green spaces. In reality, the post-war dream of thriving commuter communities had not reached this area, and it was mostly inhabited by poor families living in ageing accommodation.

To Rob's surprise, Sarah stopped at the door of an estate agents at the end of the row of shops. She reached into a large shoulder bag and pulled out a bunch of keys. She unlocked the door and stepped through, bolting it shut behind her. The parade was busy, and Rob took a seat on a bus stop bench to wait and see what could have brought the actress here at this time.

A little over ten minutes later, she stepped out and locked the door behind her. In that time, she had changed out of her outfit and into a long, pale blue t-shirt, which was at least a size too big for her, and a pair of dark blue trousers. Her sequined shoes had been replaced by dark pumps and she had removed all trace of makeup from her face. Her shoulder-length hair was now pulled back into a low ponytail.

If Rob had not been looking for her, he was not certain that he would have recognised her.

With his interest now raised, Rob followed Sarah down a series of residential roads. Five minutes after they left the estate agents, she walked up the path of a well-maintained terraced house. She stood for a moment at the door, wrestling again in her bag for her keys. Before she could find them, the door opened, and a wiry man stepped back to let her in. As she walked through the door, he grabbed her arm and pulled her towards him, planting a kiss on her left cheek. As she turned away from the man, Rob saw in profile the fear that had been simmering beneath the surface all day flash painfully across her face, before the man pushed the door closed.

CHAPTER 20

Unconvinced by Rob's concern for Sarah Fletcher, Saric preferred to spend his evening running the recording from their interview with Colin Edwards through Sense Check, hoping to rule him out of the frame so he could start narrowing down the investigation.

Saric sat at his desk. He uploaded the discussion. Saric had sort of liked Colin. He was a bit of a fussy, self-important little man, but endearing in a way. Saric's line of work put him in contact with a lot of people filled with malice. Colin was not one of these people; he seemed only to want to be noticed. Rob had agreed when they briefly discussed it at the theatre, although he also reserved his position a little by saying he thought that something was a 'bit off' with Colin.

Saric thought it likely that Colin was bothering Jane Evans because he had little else to occupy his time. Maybe Jane felt some pity for him; just because Grace would have charged him for every minute of her time did not necessarily mean Jane had the same approach. That had happened to Saric in the earlier days of his own work as a detective; sometimes he just wanted to help someone and lost sight of there being a business to run. In those days, he would berate himself when he realised he had lost sight of the commercial basis of his relationships with his clients. These days, however, he had developed a wider viewpoint, and perhaps a bit more faith in the karma of a good deed done. He was not the first businessman to develop a sense of putting something back long after he had stopped needing to worry about his own personal wealth.

Sense Check fired out the results. The display was more colourful than he had anticipated. When they spoke, Colin seemed the embodiment of grey output: trivial and irrelevant. But not so. Sense Check had brought up two logical inconsistencies, and one false factual statement, as well as a number of areas where a follow up was recommended. At first glance, it looked like Colin was in fact full of shit.

Firstly, Jane's timesheet analysis and email record showed that she almost never saw clients in person after work hours. It seemed she would happily work long into the night sometimes, but always from home. Saric wondered if that was to accommodate the dog. Colin said that he called Jane a couple of days before the last time they met to discuss a technical accounting point, and she agreed to meet after work

154

in her office. To see a client after hours in the office was exceptional for Jane, and it was not consistent with a meeting of a trivial nature.

The second thing Sense Check flagged was that Colin had stated he did not see Jane again after the evening meeting, but later in the conversation he did admit to speaking to her again about the accountancy point; " . . . the next time we spoke she was fine." These sorts of inconsistencies were typical of a false reconstruction of events.

The last key point was a cross-check issue. Colin had asserted that he had gone to the theatre in London on the day Jane was killed. He claimed to have come home via the Piccadilly Circus Underground Station that evening, but the station had been closed from 9.30 pm that night due to an 'incident'.

As he looked back on that part of the discussion, Saric also realised that Colin had not asked why he was being asked about 16th June in particular. He gave a peculiarly full answer, but he never enquired why that night. Maybe he had looked up the details of Jane's death before meeting Saric and Rob, having pre-empted the question. But why pre-empt the question? Or perhaps Colin was just bored and spent a morbid few minutes Googling the news about his ex-accountant's murder.

All rather odd, thought Saric. But the alibi would be easy enough to double check. Sense Check had corroborated the name and timings of the show he went to see. Other than a perhaps misremembered tube station, the commute times and stations stacked up. And in any case, there was nothing at all to indicate he had a reason, or the capability, to be involved in Jane's murder.

Saric sat back in his chair to mull things over and was immediately interrupted by the driveway alarm. He clicked the mouse to bring up the outside cameras. An oversized BMW was coming up his drive. Just the driver – no passengers – but it was hard to see the face from the angle. The car pulled up and Jim Callagher stepped out. As he approached the door, Saric flicked the house into full lockdown, leaving only his front room accessible. The door of the study would lock once he left it. Saric thought about arming himself but decided not to bother. In the unlikely event of hand-to-hand violence, he knew where the useful implements were in his lounge. The only real threat here anyway would be a firearm. It was ridiculous to think that Jim Callagher would turn up at his house, without concealing his identity, and shoot Saric. An open and constructive discussion seemed the likely motive.

Saric opened the door. "Hello again," he said. "Come in."

Jim followed Saric into the lounge and took a seat. He looked at Saric for a long moment, but Saric felt no need to fill the silence, which he realised was supposed to be awkward.

"You and I need to have a chat," said Jim.

"OK."

"I sent you a little message, and you sent me one back."

"I suppose so."

"Those two boys are still in the hospital. And Barry, who you glassed, wants World War Three to conclude this. So, I've done some digging and discovered that you are a more interesting character than I thought."

"I know what you've been told and by whom. Some of it's true," said Saric. He had in fact taken a call from one of his friends in the police. Jim had friends there, too.

"I was told I should drop it. Drop it! You appear in my face at my place of work. You go poking around at my accountant's office. You put two of my boys in the hospital for weeks, and they tell me I should drop it! So, I wanted to come here and meet this great detective myself. And I'm not seeing anything special. I'm not seeing any reason why I don't just come back here with a van full of boys and put you in the ground."

Jim's initial cool was starting to wear off. The way Saric looked at him as he spoke was making him feel uncomfortable. He did not feel in control of this meeting the way he had expected.

"There is a certain equilibrium required in the world, Jim. People like you are required to maintain balance. Bad people that are happy to hurt and destroy. Like bacteria, they break things down for no obvious reason, but we accept there is a place for them."

Saric leaned forward in his chair. "The world seems to need someone like you, Jim, but it does not need you in particular. It would be inconvenient for the police to put you behind bars; more hassle than it's worth, but I'm owed enough favours to make that happen."

"I doubt it," said Jim. "I call the shots around here."

Saric let the discussion drop.

"I can't allow this to end with nothing," said Jim. "Let's say I agree you are not worth the effort. So, I take your boy."

For the slightest moment, Saric did not understand, then he got it. *Rob*. Rob had never been his boy. He was his partner, his friend. And, of course, his client. Yes, still his client. Out of habit, Saric processed the thought; burn Rob and end this inconvenience. As the notion floated through his mind and got no traction, Saric was pleased to experience something unequivocal, solid, unquestioned.

"Rob is not my 'boy'," he said. "And if anyone goes near him, I will tie you up in my garage, slit your wife's throat in front of you, and pull you apart bit by bit with a pair of pliers. And then I will go after every person you know and destroy them one by one, until even saying your name out loud becomes a death sentence."

The stillness in Saric's voice as he spoke took the air out of Jim's lungs.

Saric added, "Around here, Jim, you are a someone, a tiny someone, in a tiny part of England, a tiny country. I am bigger than you. More than you in every way."

Jim was stunned. No one spoke to him like this. Even his suppliers, whom he knew had more muscle than him, treated him with respect. Or at least feigned it.

"You're a dead man," said Jim. It was all he could think of.

"You can go now," said Saric.

Jim walked out. Saric did not get up. He heard the BMW accelerate out of the drive. Saric sat back in his sofa and stared at the empty fireplace. As a child, he would stare for hours at a flickering fire. He had heard someone say that no two flames were ever the same shape. You could watch them forever and they would never repeat. In the hut in the woods, where his father took him for holidays, he learned that if you stared hard enough in total silence, you could disappear entirely, as if the world was accepting you into its arms, holding you there until it sent you back to deal with the next challenge. He still missed his dad. He would have known exactly how to deal with Jim. It would have involved pliers.

CHAPTER 21

MARCH 2016

She worked through the approach in her mind. The second part of her plan was to give them some of the Martha they wanted. She had to give them some ground, some hope of bringing her back.

It was tempting to feign an overnight conversion, just to get on with it, but there would be sceptics. She reconciled herself to a slow conversion. For several weeks, she conceded small gains to them. She started by saying amen at the end of grace, which was said before every meal that was served to her, and she built up from there. She carefully noted the looks of satisfaction, or the exchanged glances between her captors, but worked hard to ensure it didn't appear that she'd noticed. At times, when she knew they would come in and check on her, she made it look like she was praying, before badly trying to cover it up. She was taken to church services, just once a week to start with. After a while, she asked for a rosary to pray with, and then a crucifix of her own. Finally, she requested a picture of Mary, or 'The Great Mother', to hang on the wall. Their first attempt was not large enough for her needs, and they happily upgraded it to what she wanted; a larger-than-life picture of Mary's face surrounded by light. She would need that later.

She gave Martha her own character, separate from her real self. Martha moved more slowly and deliberately, and she held her shoulders differently. She played with her fingers, smiled at odd times without reason, and wore clips to keep her hair out of her face.

Over the weeks, while playing the part of Martha, she allowed Daniel to start fulfilling the role set for him. She made up thoughts that she confided in him and no one else. She explained to him how she had never felt happier than she did as a child in the Community, and how she was starting to understand why. She told him that she was little more than a child when she escaped, and that it was not really her fault. She had suffered the greatest test of faith and been exposed to the horrors of the failed and doomed society of a secular world; now she was home again at last. She held his hand, looked deep into his eyes and told him that she was starting to feel open to the new destiny that the Great Lord was calling her to.

It would soon be time for the next stage.

CHAPTER 22

Rob had stood outside Sarah's house for some time, unsure of what to do. Part of him had wanted to walk up the path and knock on the door to check she was OK, but he was doubtful whether that would achieve anything. All he had really seen was a slightly frosty exchange between a husband and wife. There was nothing particularly unusual in that. But why had she changed on her way home? And why had she look so scared?

Aware that a direct approach might do more harm than good, Rob had waited a few minutes longer and then returned home.

The next morning, still unable to shake the idea that Sarah might be in trouble, he consulted Saric. After slightly uncomfortably relaying where he had gone after speaking with Colin, to more than one raised eyebrow from his friend, he explained his concerns.

"Look, Rob, I know why you are worried, but this has nothing to do with the case. She's just a lonely woman who is not getting on with her husband. It happens. Unless you saw something more than that then it's really nothing to do with us and, to be honest, we have more important things to worry about."

"But Saric, you didn't see her. She was scared. Really scared. I'm worried about her and we can't just leave her."

Saric looked at Rob as if weighing up whether to say something that was on his mind. He took a deeper breath than was his normal pattern and his eyes softened slightly. "If it means that much to you, we can try to speak to her, but look at us, even if she is worried about something, I doubt she would open up to two strange blokes that she has barely met."

"I know, but at least we will have tried."

There was something in the resignation in Rob's voice that made Saric uneasy. His friend often reacted like this when he felt someone was at risk, and this was particularly true when that person was a woman. In others, this might have appeared to be quite patronising, but Saric knew that this aspect of Rob's character was based far more on his personal view of himself and his perceived failures than those of the people he was trying to protect. He considered for a moment whether to tell Rob about Jim's visit the previous day but concluded that until Rob was satisfied that Sarah was in no danger, it wasn't fair to burden him with the thug's threats. Saric would have liked to think that he had scared Jim off, but he knew it was far likelier that he had gone away to lick his wounds and consider how best to respond. As a result, he could not assume there would be no further retaliation for putting Jim's men in hospital, and he would need to be on his guard. However, a visit to Sarah, who was apparently completely unconnected to Jim, was unlikely to provoke anything further, so it might be a useful way to get Rob's head straight and start to diffuse the situation with Jim.

"All right, we don't have anything on this morning. It sounds like she must work at the estate agents she visited, given she has keys and out-of-hours access. How about we drop in there this morning and see if we can speak to her?"

*

As Saric and Rob walked through the door into the dusty air of the estate agents, they were greeted enthusiastically by two men, who jostled to be the first to shake their hands. Rob's disdain for estate agents was almost as strong as his hatred of cyclists, so he was pleased to disappoint them both by asking to speak to Sarah instead.

"Hi Sarah, we met briefly yesterday at the theatre. I thought your performance was outstanding," Rob lied.

A brief smile of pride flashed across the small woman's face, before it disappeared, to be replaced by something like suspicion.

"Thank you," was all she said, clearly unsure why the two men were standing in front of her.

Rob took a seat in one of the padded blue office chairs that were situated across the desk from Sarah. Saric remained standing. He could be intimidating even when he did not intend to be, and he reckoned this matter would be better dealt with by Rob alone.

As Rob sat there, he realised that he did not have a plan for what to say next. He had been so keen to get to Sarah, to check she was OK, that he did not really know what to ask. It did not seem right to jump straight into the real reason he was here.

"As I think you are aware, my colleague and I are looking into the death of an acquaintance of Colin Edwards. We saw that you are a friend of his and were wondering if you had ever met the deceased, a Mrs Jane Evans?"

166

Even before he had finished the sentence, Rob knew this was a mistake. What little colour had been present in Sarah's face drained away immediately and she stared at him for a long moment.

"I don't know anything about that. I've never met her in person."

The words poured out of her. "I'm not sure why you would ask me about that? She was just the accountant for the charity. They weren't even friends."

"I know, Mrs Fletcher, but in cases like this it's usually better to speak to as many people as we can. Can you tell me a bit about yourself? Do you live alone?"

"No, I don't. I live with my husband. But really, this has nothing to do with Colin. Please. I don't want to answer any more questions."

Saric had been standing completely still in the corner of the room but spoke now. "Thank you for your time, Mrs Fletcher, we will see ourselves out."

As the two men left the office, past the two salesman who looked equally confused and disappointed, seemingly thinking they had lost the opportunity of a sale, Saric gave Rob the kind of 'I told you so' look that he felt he probably deserved in this situation. While there was something unusual about the woman, this was not related to their case and perhaps it was better left.

Sarah watched the two men exit into the bright sunshine that poured through the large window at the front of the office. Her colleagues were looking at her strangely, shooting glances at her, which they probably thought were discrete, but which showed exactly what they were thinking. They would discuss this incident between themselves in the pub over lunch, laughing at her and wondering what she could have done to be involved with two such strange characters.

They were not bad people really, just boring. They hated each other and would willingly stab the other in the back if it meant getting a bit more commission from a sale. But every lunchtime they disappeared off together to the pub to pretend to be best friends and share half-invented stories of their successes with women, the cars they were going to buy with their next big commission and whose football team was most likely to win the league. Half of it was lies, of course, but they kept doing it day after day because that is what successful salesmen are supposed to do.

Sarah was never invited to those lunches but that was all right; she did not need their approval. Instead, she lifted the receiver of her desk phone and dialled a number from memory.

"It's me, I need to see you . . . No, today . . . I'll be at the café at 12.30."

She had to keep their conversations brief in the office. Her colleagues sometimes bumped into her husband at those ridiculous networking events that the town put on for 'the business community'.

At 12.20 pm, Sarah got up from her desk, picked up her bag and left the office, locking the door behind her. Her colleagues had already left for their lunch hour, so the office would be empty for a while, but as no one was checking on them, it did not really matter. The café was a longer walk than was strictly necessary to find lunch in town, but it was quiet, and they were unlikely to be disturbed or recognised. It was a shabby place that did most of its business serving breakfast to electricians and plumbers before work. Come lunchtime, it tried to transform into a trendy café, but the laminated menus and plastic seats meant it did not quite achieve this aim, and as a result they were often the only people in there.

Sarah ordered a black coffee whilst she waited for Colin. It was the usual story; he would be late and blame his workload and the unreasonable finance director, who expected him to do three people's work.

He was ten minutes late by the time he pushed his way through the door. He hurried over to the table, squeezing himself between carelessly arranged chairs. As he reached her, he hesitated for just a moment, their usual familiarity disturbed by a public setting. He pulled out the chair opposite her, sat down heavily and started playing with the corner of the menu.

"Hi," she said. He made her nervous although she could not articulate why. "How was your morning?"

"Oh, you know, the usual. Too much to do and not enough staff to get it done. And the ones I do have are next to useless. Did I tell you that the girl they gave me as an apprentice wants a week off in December to visit her family in Spain? She knows it's our busiest time, but she says all her relatives are going for Christmas, so I can hardly say no, can I?"

Sarah was glad when the waitress came to their table to take their order. He had told her this story before, and while she enjoyed hearing about his work, it could sometimes be a little tiring, particularly when she did not agree with his point of view. There was no use in trying to persuade him that perhaps a week with her family over Christmas would be a nice break for the apprentice. After all, she was only eighteen, and being away from family over the festive season must be terrible. She had tried to take the opposite view on some other trivial work matter once, and it had resulted in a twenty-minute explanation from Colin on why he was much better qualified to understand the intricacies of the situation than she was. So, this time, she simply sat quietly and nodded in the right places.

"I'll have a bacon sandwich on white bread, with some chips on the side, and Sarah would like tuna salad on brown, please. And a mug of tea, too. Thank you."

When they first met, Sarah had found it endearing that Colin would order food for her; it was nice that he cared and she liked the attention, but as time had gone on, she wondered if it was not a little patronising, as if she was not able to make up her own mind or converse with the waitress for herself. But she was happy with tuna, so she did not raise it with him – it seemed to make him happy and that was nice.

Once the waitress was safely out of earshot, she explained about the visit from Rob and Saric.

"What did they want?"

"I'm not sure really, it was a bit strange. They just arrived and asked how I was. I told them to leave so they did."

"Did they ask about the accountant?"

"Yes, they asked if I knew her, but it was like they didn't really care about the answer. I don't know what to make of it, but I thought you would want to know, as they were talking to you yesterday."

"Did they threaten you?" His question came out of nowhere and was not what she had expected.

"What? No! Nothing like that, they were perfectly polite, actually. That big guy with the accent, he's a bit strange. I wouldn't want to get on the wrong side of him, but the other one is lovely, he seems more like a teacher than a detective."

"Well, maybe he should be, they don't seem very professional to me. Very unusual pair, and I'm not sure if it's only a business partnership, if you know what I mean."

Sarah did, but she could not see why Colin cared either way, so she sipped her coffee and tried to nod in a way that would encourage him to keep talking but move on to a different subject.

"Anyway, don't talk to them again without me there. In fact, I might go and give that chap a piece of my mind. He can't just barge in and demand to speak to you like that."

Sarah tried to imagine what a confrontation between Colin and the big detective might look like. Colin was round and soft and full of words, while the other man was chiselled and solid and seemed to rarely say anything. But anyway, there was no need for any of this.

"I'm sure that's not necessary, like I said, they didn't seem interested and we would not want to draw any more attention, would we? And there's Andrew to consider."

Colin winced at the sound of her husband's name. They had never met, but Colin hated the man, and recoiled whenever Sarah mentioned him. In any case, it was best that the police did not start poking around.

"I'm sure I can persuade him to stop bothering you." Colin was sitting up straight now, his broad chest stretched wide, while his fingers gripped the edges of the table.

"I think it might be better if we left it for now. Don't forget we have the rest of the performances to worry about. Tell me, what do you think we could improve for the next one?"

Their food arrived and Sarah spent the rest of her lunch hour listening to a minute-by-minute dissection of the show and each performer's flaws. Colin was a remarkable man in many ways, and it was lovely just to spend time in the company of someone who enjoyed being near her.

CHAPTER 23

The next day was a Saturday, and a day off for Rob.

Since joining up with Saric, the working week had lost its relevance; there was either work to do or there wasn't. There was a time when losing a weekend to work would have been a significant issue for Rob, and he would fight hard to keep them clear. These days, though, he preferred his days to be occupied. But today was different; he had a social engagement to go to. For many years, the family barbeque had been a big event, and this year it was his little brother's turn to host. He would have to attend on his own again, as his wife and son would not be around for it. Saric had also received an invitation from Rob's father, and he'd said he would come along for a bit.

The weather was playing its part in creating the right sense of occasion; a clear blue sky allowed the bright sun to dominate, with only faint wisps of cloud scattered around, as if placed there purely for visual effect. There was a pleasant heat in the day, which was slowing the pace of the people of West Sussex.

After a breakfast of eggs and carbs, Rob digested it in front of the television, before heading out for a run. People were out in their gardens; mowing their lawns, fiddling around with their borders or just standing around drinking coffee and thinking about what job to do next. Rob jogged past a man, aged around his late forties, filling his people carrier with rubbish to take to the tip. He was struggling with an old, floral-patterned armchair and Rob wondered why no one was around to help him, though he did not think to stop himself.

Rob ran for longer than usual. Although the day was getting hot, he kept on going, as it was preferable to sitting around at home waiting for it to be time to go out. He was exhausted by the time he arrived home and stood on the path to his front door with his hands on his knees, sucking in great gulps of air. Maybe he had overdone it a bit. As he stood there, the mother and toddler who lived next door left their house to get in the car. The mother was blonde, like his wife Helen, and a similar build. The two women had been friends. When she saw Rob, she pulled her son closer and hurried to the car, trying to make it look like she had not seen him. That relationship had been destroyed, along with so many others, years ago. Rob had gone through a difficult time.

I'm doing better now, he thought, but as he tried to steady himself to walk into his house, he glanced at his neighbour once more. He saw his own wife in her, and his own son in her boy; the way she looked at him was the way he wished he could look at his own. His head was spinning. As he started to walk, his legs gave way and he stumbled into an overgrown bush. He lay there for several moments, allowing the branches to hurt him as they spiked into his body.

I need to cut this back for when they get home, he thought, before collecting himself and half crawling back into his house. He thought his neighbour might have seen him, which would have looked a little odd, but she had seen worse.

He sat on his sofa, comforted that he would have a while to recover before getting ready to go out, which was good purely because it killed some time.

The invitation said to arrive 'from 2pm'. He knew that meant his brother would be expecting him somewhere around 2.30 pm. He also knew that Saric would struggle with such a vague instruction. As he had not asked Rob what time he was actually supposed to be there, he assumed his father had edited Saric's invite to make it easier to follow.

Rob made an effort when he got dressed. Not for his own sake, but out of respect for his family. He knew what to expect; most of the people there would be smartly dressed, especially the women. The nice earrings would be out, along with the strappy tops and the heels. The men would be expected to have a collar, although clearly this was never instructed. Polo shirts would be acceptable, but Rob went for a plain white, short-sleeved shirt. He had always been in reasonable shape, and confident in the way he looked. Although he was in the best physical condition of his life, the interest of a woman was best avoided. His old, confident charm was something he would turn on as required, but he was not sure whether it was actually him anymore.

Despite himself, he glanced in the mirror before he left. "You're a failure," he said to himself, "and soon, you're going to have to accept that you have failed."

He was about to argue back but snapped himself out of it. This was not a place to go to today; today he would hold it together.

He pulled into the drive of his brother John's house. The man had done well for himself, or at least, he had done what everyone had expected him to do. He was a lawyer, as was his wife, although she was on a career break to raise children. They only had one child for now, but Rob suspected they had been trying for a second for a while. At one time, he might have talked to John about that, but only after they had both got drunk. Rob no longer drank at family events, and he and his brother's diaries never quite seemed to work out for getting together just the two of them, so the opportunity never arose. Rob knew that was his job as big brother, and he hoped his younger sibling had someone he could talk to. He could confide in Dad, of course, but as he always supported their decisions and backed his sons to achieve whatever they put their minds to, he was not great for offering another point of view or challenging them. What he was good for was offering hugs when all seemed lost, as Rob knew too well. Rob would seek his Dad out as soon as he walked into the party, and he would let him take care of everything.

He walked round the side gate, which was off the latch, and into the back garden. The barbeque playlist was filling the garden with upbeat pop music. Rob took a deep breath. To avoid memories, he only listened to new music as a rule, although he was confident John would have at least made sure that the song accompanying his first dance at his wedding would be absent from the track list. Later, someone would turn the music up, the heels would be kicked off and people would dance in

179

the twilight. Little kids would be swung in the air and aunties and uncles and cousins and friends and grandchildren would celebrate the simple joy of being together in the sunshine.

"Rob!" It was Cousin Patrick's wife, Jemma. This side of the family seemed to be half a generation ahead, placing Patrick and his rather wonderful wife around ten years Rob's senior. She held his shoulders, looked him straight in the eye and then kissed his cheek. "How are you, darling?"

"I'm really well," said Rob, "you know."

She gazed at him briefly, as if about to say something important. Instead, she squeezed his arm, "Looking good! You've been working out. Patrick, why don't you look after yourself like little Rob here, eh?"

Patrick broke away from the conversation he was half having in a small group. "You're going to have to stop working out, Rob, you're making the rest of us look small." He smiled a big smile. "Come on, big man, let's get you a beer."

Rob accepted the offer, knowing he would make this beer last.

"You still playing rugby?" Cousin Patrick asked.

"Not for a while," said Rob. In fact, he had stopped playing four years ago, having embarrassed himself after arguably starting a fight in a curry house. He came out of it without a scratch on him, but his scrum half had spent a night in hospital. The club would probably have had him back, with suitable apologies, but Rob had taken it as a sign that he needed to leave that all behind. He missed it sometimes, but he did not trust himself to compete within the rules anymore.

Rob knew where to go next with Cousin Patrick. "Is that your M3 in the drive?"

"Ha! How did you guess? It sure is. What a machine. Without a doubt, it's the best car I have ever owned, and you know I've had a few. You should feel it. I had your dad in it a few weeks ago, and even he agreed it has a kick. And you know what he's like with cars!"

Before he had met Rob's mother, Rob's dad had been a semi-professional rally driver. He knew cars. Rob was pretty sure his dad was being polite about the M3. He had never heard him say anything positive about a rear-wheel-drive car before. At least, not one built since the late '80s.

"Where is Dad?" Rob asked.

"Surrounded by the kids, of course!" Patrick pointed across the garden.

Rob's dad was in goal, whilst five or six children, aged from four to twelve, raced around with a ball taking shots.

Ollie should be here, thought Rob.

"Uncle Geoff!" shouted Patrick. Rob wished he had not, as eyes flicked in their direction. Rob's dad looked up and, seeing that his son was there, excused himself from the game with promises for his imminent return, and walked across to them.

"The big man's here," said Patrick. "Sorry, I promised Jemma a drink." He walked off.

"Hi, Dad."

"Hello, my son," said his father. "You OK?"

"I'm OK."

"Good."

"John got everything under control?"

"Don't be ridiculous. No one could get this rabble under control. Auntie Jean was asked to bring a dessert and brought two salads instead, Patrick was supposed to bring baguettes and bought twenty bottles of Stella, John forgot to put the oven on, so the chicken's going to be late, and poor old Briony still seems to think any of us give a damn!"

They both laughed.

Briony was John's wife. Rob loved her because John loved her, but otherwise they would never have become close. Rob considered her to be a shallow thinker. She was intelligent, well read and academic, but she did not seem to want to direct any energy into the deeper meaning of things. Rob knew there was nothing wrong with that. In a way, he envied her, and maybe would have been happier if he could have become comfortable with the ordinary. But Helen was not ordinary, and he loved her in a way he did not think he could explain to Briony. Or maybe that was just nonsense.

"Are you working on something at the moment?" Geoff asked.

"Yes," said Rob.

"Interesting?"

"Yes. Saric's got Sense Check to run real-time voice recognition. It's proving to be pretty useful."

"Eh?"

"It's a computer thing."

"Oh, right."

"Got the usual crowd today?" asked Rob.

"Yes, the usual crowd. It's safe here, you know. Just have a good time. Everyone knows who you are. Get me if you need me." Geoff paused for a moment. "Saric will be here at exactly 3.30 pm." Rob laughed.

"Any news?" asked Geoff.

"Not for a while."

"Well, something will turn up soon."

Rob looked at his dad. He would never give up.

"Yes, something will turn up, Dad."

John interrupted. "Hello, big brother. Come on, it's mingling time."

Rob spent the next half hour nodding and making noises of agreement as the small talk flowed.

At 3.30 pm exactly, the doorbell rang. Only Saric would keep to the formality of the doorbell, Rob decided, and so it was.

Geoff showed Saric through the house into the kitchen. He put the two bottles of wine he had brought at the back of a kitchen cupboard, instead of onto the kitchen surface with the rest of the booze.

Knowing that Saric would have selected his offering from his cellar, Rob was pleased to think that John and Briony would enjoy it between them, maybe in front of a good film of an evening, instead of having Aunty Jean gulping it down oblivious of its fine qualities.

Saric nodded at Rob, and was swept away by Geoff, presumably for an update.

The smell of barbequed meat was now rich in the air around the patio. Men hovered around. Rob was not really hungry, but out of instinct he gravitated in that direction. John was there, along with a member of Briony's family whom Rob could not remember meeting before, and his son, who looked to be somewhere around fourteen years old. The adults were talking.

"Hello," said Rob to the boy.

"Hello."

"Who are you, then?" he tried hard to sound friendly.

"I'm James."

James's dad broke off from his conversation with John. "Hi, my wife is Briony's oldest school friend. They've known each other since they were seven."

He offered his hand to shake. By instinct, Rob took the man's body language in. He was being genuinely friendly, and Rob liked him straight away.

Turning back to the boy, Rob said, "Nice to meet you, James, how are you, then?"

"I'm good, thanks."

"Oh." The conversation seemed to have run its course.

"He's fourteen," offered his dad as an explanation.

"I see," said Rob. "I better say hello to Saric," he added and walked off.

By five o'clock, enough alcohol had been consumed for the party to have found full swing. The mums had given up swapping stories about how well their children were getting on at school or hockey club, or in comparison to the national average, and were getting more interested in who had gotten fat, and whether everyone had heard about the mother that might have to go to rehab.

By six o'clock, the children were starting to get hungry again. Piles of cold meat were offered up, along with mountains of salad, all of which was largely ignored in favour of hot dog rolls and butter. The younger children were starting to tire, as were some of the older generation. Cries of, "Don't do that" and "Will you just stop!" started to become more regular.

Little Brandon, just three years old, ran full speed into a garden chair. He spun sideways off it onto the grass. The surrounding adults held their breath to see if damage had been done. Geoff, the nearest adult, returned him to his feet. Poor Brandon, unsure if he had been hurt or not, looked around in panic for his mum. She was already running up the garden in patterned flip flops to the rescue. She was letting out a gulping noise and had such a look of fear on her face that Brandon could be in no doubt he was on the edge of death. He burst into tears, much to Geoff's surprise, and stood screaming until Mother scooped him up. She held him close, looking left and right, as if there was something else that needed to happen next, but there wasn't, so she just stood there until Brandon knew for sure that his mother had saved him and the tears stopped.

What a palaver, Geoff thought.

Rob thought the same.

Saric was mystified by the whole thing.

The incident seemed to punctuate the evening.

Rob looked at Saric.

"Are you OK for our evening appointment?" Saric asked him.

"Yes, sure," Rob answered.

Rob hugged those that wanted hugs, shook a few hands and kissed a few cheeks.

Saric shook Geoff's hand, and then John's, expressed his genuine thanks for being invited and the two of them left. Although Saric had come by taxi, and Rob had driven, without discussing it, Saric got into the driver's seat and drove Rob home. Saric sat with him until bedtime, with the TV on in the background, and then a taxi came to take him home.

Rob, as promised, went straight to bed, even though he knew he would lay awake for hours yet, alone with his thoughts. He thought of his dad. He wished he had not let him down so badly.

CHAPTER 24

SEPTEMBER 2016

For some years, she had applied everything she had learned to help people. Now it was time to apply herself to self-preservation. In Daniel, they had given her everything she needed. He was going to be her way out of here.

She was going to take control of his mind.

When she had first resolved herself to this plan, she was uncomfortably aware that it went against everything she believed in. After all, she had spent many years devoting herself to helping people free themselves from negative thoughts that were trapping them into bad habits, unhealthy lifestyles or miserable lives. Every time she helped a patient medically, or a client therapeutically, move their lives in a positive direction, she felt a profound sensation of peace. She believed that she had found a way to channel the challenges of her own life to benefit others, and this was important to her. She wanted to be a good person and measured her success by how she helped others.

But as she learned more about the brain and the mind, she also became aware that the same knowledge can take you to dark places.

In practice, the malicious application of the knowledge she shared was channelled mostly to the mundane area of selling crap to people who did not need it. But it was definitely not all harmless. Behind the scenes of politics, teams of people spent their careers coming up with more and more ingenious ways of promoting blatant lies – and getting away with it – as if it were all a game.

Perhaps it is, Martha thought. But if governments across the world running the planet based on what lies they could get away with was a game, there were more overtly sinister applications. She had once come across a course for single men who wanted to learn how to manufacture a one-night stand, using some horribly manipulative techniques.

She would have liked to wage a campaign against them, but she did not really know how to start that, and with a busy life she soon forgot all about it. As she thought about it now, she wondered if these types of courses still existed in the world of online dating, which, from talking to some of her friends, seemed to remove the need for manipulation on either side. She didn't really understand how anyone could live their life like that, but perhaps that was a hangover from her childhood.

If she was fully honest with herself, and she was, she recognised that there had been moments when she had applied a little manipulation herself. But it had only ever been for minor conveniences; jumping a queue in the post office with a bored, hungry toddler starting to act up, or making quite sure that she would get a refund at customer services for a dress she had lost the receipt for. But that was fine, wasn't it? She had also taught her husband some of the basics, which he had picked up well, and he agreed these little concessions were not a problem.

"Look at all the good you're doing!" he would say. "I think you are up on the moral equation." He would smile, and she would feel OK about it.

Now she was preparing to turn that on its head. She needed assistance to get her and her son home, and no one here was going to give it to her willingly. Instead, she would have to force one of them to do what she needed.

Daniel was the perfect candidate. He was a product of the Community. He did not understand doubt, or being unsure, or equivocating. She would take him to the edge of an entirely new reality, and then push him over. And then – she felt sure – once there, he would accept that world completely. And in the new world she had created for him, she would be the one true voice, and he would be hers.

It hurt her to think about it. She had promised never to use her knowledge in this way. By the time she'd made use of him, she didn't know if he could be returned to the world he knew, or a happy new one. She didn't even know if she would get the chance to try and help him recover. He had to be disposable. It was brutal. Cruel, even. She held the thought of her son in her mind and answered the question she was grappling with. Yes. She could do it.

There was a knock at her door, followed by a pause, which meant it was Daniel.

"Come in," Martha said. She was sitting at her desk, with the Bible open in front of her. She liked to leave it open on Ezekiel 25:17. It amused her that she was the only person in the Community who knew it was most famous across the world for being the speech given by Samuel L. Jackson's gangster character in *Pulp Fiction*.

"It's time for your exercise," he said. She was taken into the grounds for a workout once a day. "I thought I could jog with you."

"Yes," she said, "thank you." She paused for a moment and held his gaze. She easily mirrored his breathing pattern. She stood up without breaking eye contact and took on the look of someone in deep and profound thought.

First, she would elicit confusion to help his mind freewheel a little. To do this, she would construct sentences that almost sounded like they made sense. With his mind grasping to decipher them, she would add a suggestion in a normal language pattern.

"Daniel," she said. "I want you to understand something very important. It isn't that there is anything important for me not to tell you, only that I wonder whether if you were to concentrate, if you wouldn't be able to *believe what I tell you*."

She changed tone very slightly to deliver the suggestion. Daniel stood in silence for a moment trying to catch up. She took a step to the left and positioned herself between him and the picture of Mary that hung on the wall. She turned her face to match her expression.

"Look at me, Daniel," she said. "I think that if you were to start to wonder what it is, you would find you already know. It might be only later when you look back that you start to realise what you know to be

194

true. You have been such a good student of the Great Lord. If he has chosen you to hear his word, you may wonder about the first thing you will feel that will let you know . . . *you are ready to hear his word*."

Daniel was transfixed.

"I have heard the truth," she went on, "it is me, Marytha."

She had practised the pronunciation of the Mary/Martha conflation. It was important for Daniel's mind to let it slip through, and she was pleased that he seemed not to have heard it consciously.

"*You are feeling this feeling now* to know that you and I are at one in this, with the Great Mother."

That was enough for now. She started backing him out.

Changing the tone of her voice again to a normal, for Martha, conversational tone, she added, "I would like to talk about this with you again, I think *it will be interesting for you to consider this* with me later. Well, *look at me*–" she broke eye contact "–I'm waffling on and we need to go for a jog. What route do you want to take today?"

He stumbled over his words for a moment and was pleased to grasp hold of the question, for which he had an answer.

"I thought round the lake would be nice."

"OK," she said, "let's go, then."

She thought that had gone quite well as a starter.

CHAPTER 25

Rob and Saric spent the next morning at their desks following up on various elements of the case that were still outstanding. Many of the points seemed inconsequential on their own but experience had taught them that these were the kinds of points that could make the case.

Rob spent over an hour on the phone to a rather unhelpful general manager at the golf club where Tony Spencer had claimed to be on the night of the murder. The manager seemed to think that information about who might have been at the hotel that night was confidential, in the same way as a person's medical records, or what they had confessed to their priest, might be. Eventually, Rob was able to impress upon the poor man the importance of the case, and of Saric's connection to several influential members of the club, and he was able to establish that Tony Spencer was indeed at the event. He'd had more than one too many and caused embarrassment by throwing himself at a young and rather attractive member of the bar team. From the way the manager was talking, Rob thought it likely that given a chance, the manager might be only too pleased to embarrass himself in front of this young lady too.

But at least it had made Tony's presence stand out in the manager's mind in sufficient detail that he was able to corroborate that the accountant was at the event all night and in no state to go anywhere but home when he was bundled into the taxi.

Saric's morning was no more fruitful. He had decided to try and close off the open matters relating to Jane Evans's disgruntled client and her ex-employee.

Sense Check had tracked down the man who had sued Jane's firm two years previously. He was now living happily in a villa near Madrid with his wife, having retired there at the start of the year. A quick call enabled Saric to eliminate him from any suspicion. He did not even remember Jane by name and the matter had been resolved fairly amicably on both sides.

The ex-employee was more difficult. He was easy to find on a professional networking site, as he was now working in a similar role at a different accountancy firm. He answered the call immediately, which surprised Saric, as it was a Sunday and he was calling a work line, but he shut down when Saric mentioned the reason for his call. Working for a rival firm meant he had heard about Jane's murder, but he refused to tell Saric anything until he asked him what his new employer felt about his dismissal from his previous job. At this point, realising that Saric would be more than willing to correct his oversight of omitting to mention his reason for leaving, he became completely compliant, explaining that he had been entertaining his new girlfriend at home on the night of the murder. He was able to describe, in a little too much detail for Saric in some areas, what they had done that evening, but the takeaway order and the film they had bought on Sky were verifiable. Ultimately, Saric was happy that there was enough evidence to eliminate him.

Rob sat back in his chair and stretched both arms behind him, trying to ease out the tension of a morning spent sitting. "I realise that eliminating three potential suspects should feel like progress," he said, "but I don't feel like we are any further forward."

"We know more now than we did this morning," Saric said matter-of-factly.

"I know, but we never really thought those guys had anything to do with it, did we?"

"Perhaps not, but we have more facts now. The pool of potential suspects is smaller."

Saric sometimes wondered if it would be possible to accrue enough information about enough people that Sense Check would be able to solve crimes independently. In principle, it should be possible. If all data were available to it then it would know where everybody was at all times. Maybe it could even use past patterns to predict future actions. He had raised the idea with Rob once, on a particularly sunny afternoon in a pub garden. Rob had disagreed entirely, believing that people were capable of exercising sufficient free will that it was not possible to predict their actions. Privately, Saric held this conversation ready to pursue again at another time. He knew he would never achieve that level of detail and the prediction algorithms would be ludicrously complex, but in theory at least, it should be possible, and one day he would persuade Rob of this.

"Why don't we break for lunch? I'll cook if you like."

"Sorry, mate, I've got to give Dad a lift to collect his car from John's house. He left it there yesterday and I said I'd drop him round there to save him getting the bus. I'll only be a couple of hours. I hope that's OK?"

"Yes, of course. Sorry, I didn't realise you had plans. Why don't we leave things for today? It is Sunday after all."

"Sounds good to me. I've been meaning to get out into the garden for ages, so maybe I'll make a start on that." Even as he said it, Rob knew he would not.

After Rob left, Saric moved to his kitchen to make himself some lunch. The kitchen was a relatively large room, which stretched across the whole width of the ground floor. Floor-to-ceiling glass along the back wall let light stream in from the well-tended garden. He had designed the layout of the house to suit him exactly, and as he had never accumulated items in the same way as other people, his kitchen looked the same as it had on the day he chose the design. Handmade wooden doors paired with stainless steel created a beautiful but functional space that Saric enjoyed preparing food in.

The smell of fried mackerel was enticing. When he'd first come to the south of England, it had taken him a while to find a fishmonger he could trust, but once he had found the little shack at Lancing, he had become one of their best customers. He always bought fish whole, filleting them only just before they were cooked. The plain boiled rice was ready, and he had a wedge of lemon prepared to squeeze the moment the perfectly seasoned fish hit his plate. In Saric's mind, it was perhaps the worst possible time to be interrupted, and it was exactly when his phone rang.

He looked at the number, hoping it was someone he could call back later, but no such luck. It was Deputy Chief Stephens, which meant it was relevant to the case, and that had to come first, even before perfectly cooked mackerel. He sighed and took the call.

"Hi Saric," said the Deputy Chief. "I promised to update you on the Evans case when we got something. Well, we are closing in on it."

"Go on," said Saric.

"We got clearance for the IT guys to pull records. Turns out your man Mr Evans had plenty of motive to go with his look-through alibi. We've brought him in."

"You arrested him?"

"Yes, we've got enough on him now. I'd like to get some forensics, or some solid evidence to put him right there that night, but it looks like he was a combination of smart and lucky."

"What was the big break, then?"

"The phone records tell a great story. On one chain he's got his mistress, poor girl, badgering him about 'next steps' and needing to see him 'go through with it'. On the other hand, he's literally told his wife he wants her dead. Looks like he was building up to this for some time. It's textbook. We just need to squeeze him enough to fall over on his story and we'll have him pouring out a confession."

"So, nothing to support the alibi, then?"

"Nothing. Come on, Saric – 'my dog got lost' – it's practically 'my dog ate my homework'. You don't buy that, do you?"

"Hmmm. Not sure."

"You know as well as I do that the odds are on the husband from the start," said the Deputy Chief, "we'll get him, you mark my words."

"I'm not sure," said Saric.

"Well, I am sure," said the Deputy Chief, "not absolutely certain, but pretty sure. You know that I tell you what I can on these things, but there is other evidence that points to him. That girlfriend was trouble. Not the pretty little thing that she would have you believe. Of course, he says he knew nothing about that, but he would, wouldn't he? I can hear you aren't convinced, Saric, but you should have asked him about the girl. I reckon you've lost your chance now; we'll be charging him soon."

Saric gazed at his lunch, which, removed from the pan, was starting to go cold, and let out a little sigh. "I might have to remove Callagher," he said, changing the subject.

"That would be a bloody nuisance; we've already cleared up after you once. Look, we keep Jim under control. He's not the worst operator we've had in this area. Do me a favour, will you; find another way. If you want us to have a word let me know. And if you really are going to do something bold, then for God's sake let me know first so we can keep it tight. And don't get silly, you know there's only so much I can do. And keep Rob out of it, I can't extend my reach to every bugger you pal up with."

"All right, I'll have a think," said Saric, and he meant it. "I haven't exhausted my investigation on the Evans case, and I'm not convinced the husband is your man. I'll let you know if I get something important, and tell me if Mr Evans gives you something, won't you? And brace yourself for the lawyers, I doubt there's anything he'll spend money on as happily as himself."

With that they ended the call. Saric ate his lunch, wondering how much better it would have been without the interruption.

As he ate, he also reflected on the case. There was a lot about it which was bothering him. Phillip's alibi was not strong, and the spouse was usually a good bet in these circumstances, but the lack of clarity made him uneasy about the police's approach.

It wasn't that Phillip couldn't have done it. He had all but admitted that he was stuck in an unhappy marriage and looking for a way out, but equally there was no proof that he had, and too much that did not quite make sense.

Firstly, an unhappy marriage was not sufficient motive for a normal person to kill someone, and while Phillip was not the most likeable man Saric had ever met, he was the archetype of normal – so why not just get a divorce? The way the Deputy Chief described it, the police were resting a lot on the texts from the other woman, but from the way Phillip had talked about her at their initial meeting, she was nothing more than a small distraction from the monotony of his day-to-day life. She was nothing serious and certainly not someone for whom Phillip cared sufficiently to commit murder. A middle-aged man having an affair with someone who worked for him was hardly a new story. Saric pondered what Stephens had just said about her. It wasn't quite enough to give him the full picture, but there was more to this woman than met the eye; he wondered if they should meet her, and whether the police already had.

Next, the police were contending that Phillip travelled all the way to Reading to kill his own wife. Even if a reasonable motive could be found, and Saric wasn't sure that this was the case, why would he do that and expose himself to more risk of being found, when an accident at home would have been far easier to engineer and much less risky? In another scenario, with another cast, Saric could just about have believed that Phillip travelled to Reading to surprise Jane and was somehow provoked to unpremeditated violence, but this seemed improbable given the state of their marriage, and he would have been visiting her at a public place, so surely someone would have seen him.

Trying to prove a negative was always difficult, so Saric decided to focus on proving who had done it. It would be better for the business if the person they found was not Phillip, but Saric would be satisfied either way. The truth was more important than customer satisfaction.

On this side of the equation, his primary question was what the fluid the police had found at the scene was, and how did it interact with the way Jane had been killed? If it was important enough to keep back from the public, it must have some impact on the case. It was strange that the Deputy Chief had not mentioned it as part of the evidence they had against Phillip. It was more likely that it didn't help to incriminate him, and so was being ignored. This was an unresolved point that needed further work.

Aside from Phillip, Tony seemed like a dead end. While he certainly had a few skeletons to hide, he had a strong alibi that had been verified by too many reliable sources. Jim was a different story. At this point, Saric knew he needed to step outside his own bias against the man and examine the facts. Jim was a criminal, capable in both emotional and practical terms of murder, or at least of arranging for a murder to happen. As a result of the latter part of that statement, his alibi was worthless; if he had arranged for Jane's murder, of course he would make sure he had an alibi when it was happening. It was possible to stretch the facts to give him motive to kill Jane; she was close to discovering at least some of his financial crimes, or perhaps she already had. But Jim must know that the police would not come after him for those, and Saric suspected they were probably protecting him from worse. Was that enough for Jim to order a murder? Saric thought it possible but unlikely. More than anything else with Jim, the style of Jane's death bothered Saric. Jim had a style. It was not the most sophisticated that Saric had ever come across, but it was consistent. It was important to Jim to be seen to be in charge. He was the sort of man who would order his thugs to attack in the middle of the street in the early evening, and who would come alone to Saric's own house wanting to send a message that could not be missed. He was the boss, and anyone who tried to interfere with that would be dealt with. This was the opposite of quietly suffocating someone in an anonymous hotel room. It was not impossible that the murderer was Jim, but it was definitely unlikely.

Saric made a mental note of the points to follow up on. The most immediate aspect was to find out what the fluid was and why it was important. If the police would not tell him then he needed another way into that, and he thought he might know of just the person. They also needed to speak to Phillip to follow up on any points that might prove his alibi. This could not be done until the police had finished with him, so it would have to wait. They ought to double check the inconsistencies with Colin's statement. This was only really for completeness, but Saric liked all ends to be tidied up. In addition to this, there were a few follow ups on the other, more mundane cases that needed to be dealt with. While Phillip's case was their only active matter, there were always loose ends to tidy up on recently closed matters.

Saric put in a call to a contact in the police lab that might be able to help him with the fluid identification. He did not like going behind the Deputy Chief's back like this, but it was important, and now the police thought they had their man, the information was even less likely to be forthcoming. The lab tech owed Saric a favour, and while Saric was reluctant to call it in, he saw no other way. His contact was busy so Saric left him a voicemail asking him to call back urgently.

Saric thought for a moment about what to do next. Until he knew more about that liquid, he felt that his efforts could be better placed elsewhere. Too much depended on that evidence. His mind hovered over an older case for a minute. He was highly efficient and almost always got to the right conclusion, but until now this other case had beaten him. He should look again at the evidence. Perhaps there would be a fresh connection now that Sense Check's new programming was running. He opened the files saved on a secure drive on his computer. The additional levels of security were needed on this one to keep them away from everyone but him. The consequences were too big to have the files in the open.

Sense Check was brilliant, but it was not instant; there was just too much data out there. And every time it ran an old case it had to cross check everything again, to protect against changes to the already established facts. There was a time when that would not have been necessary, facts were just facts, but in the online world even they changed, and noticing that could sometimes be the key.

Saric's unresolved case was difficult and it made him twitchy. There was too much resting on whether this time would be the time that the connection was found. To give himself something to do, he picked up the phone and found himself dialling Grace. But before the call could connect, his driveway alarm sprang to life. Someone was approaching the front door.

CHAPTER 26

Colin Edwards ignored the doorbell and hammered on the heavy wooden door with his fist. Saric observed him passively through the camera. The slightly distorted view rounded the image somewhat and made Colin look even heavier than he was in reality. He was angry. Which was interesting.

Thinking that it would do no harm to leave his visitor outside for a few moments, and happy to delay whatever annoying confrontation was coming his way, Saric mentally reviewed the conversation in the theatre bar. It had been a standard witness interview, nothing more. Nothing in that conversation would have made Colin this angry.

It was also interesting that the card Saric had given to Colin included a phone number but not an office address – Saric's clients were told where to come when they booked an appointment. This meant that Colin had taken steps to find his address. This was available online easily enough, but the fact that Colin had bothered to find it instead of calling was worthy of note.

Overall, Saric thought that whatever Colin had come to discuss was important to him, but even so, he did not bother to take the same precautions as he had when Jim had arrived uninvited.

The front door was barely halfway open before Colin pushed his way through. Saric allowed this.

"You took your time. I've been waiting out here for ages," he blustered. He was red faced and breathing heavily. There was no car in the driveway. He had walked here.

"Apologies, I wasn't expecting any visitors today, Mr Edwards." Saric made his best attempt at friendly charm and thought how proud Rob would be of him for not leaving the other man standing on the doorstep.

"What do you think you are doing, invading Sarah's work like that? The poor woman is terrified that you are coming after her. She has nothing to do with Jane Evans at all. I don't think they have even met."

The words fell out of Colin's mouth as if he had been working on them all the way to Saric's door.

This was an interesting development.

"Mr Edwards, would you like to come into my office and sit down?" Saric's offer was partly an attempt to diffuse Colin's anger and partly because Saric was concerned for his blood pressure. Colin made a big show of refusing the offer, saying that they could discuss the matter where they were, but he followed Saric to the office anyway. As Saric sat behind his large wooden desk, Colin ignored Rob's three coloured chairs and took a seat in a comfortable armchair, which was normally Rob's space. Saric smiled to himself. Whatever test you set, someone always found a way around it.

Again, Saric thought that it would be helpful to make the other man wait slightly, just to help ensure the right power dynamic in this conversation, which he wanted to take place on his terms. He did not like people turning up uninvited and demanding an audience, so a little discomfort would do no harm.

He made a show of closing down a couple of screens on his computer and, as he did so, he quietly turned on Sense Check's listening function. Rob would not like him to record Colin without his consent, but Saric considered this to be a legitimate action if it would help with the case in any way. If Colin had nothing to hide then there was no problem, and if he did then he had no right to privacy. In any case, one of the benefits of operating outside the usual structures was that he did not have to concern himself with the admissibility of evidence or whether his actions met the terms of any ethical code other than his own.

After a few moments, he looked the older man straight in the eye. "Mr Edwards, my colleague and I met with Mrs Fletcher at her office because there were a couple of points we wanted to clarify with her. We did not invade her office; we spoke for about five minutes before leaving. Two of her colleagues were present for the whole conversation."

Colin looked away. He had prepared for an argument, not Saric's distant demeanour. "She has nothing to do with this."

"We did not suggest that she did; we were just interested in her view of things."

"What things?"

"That is not really your concern, Mr Edwards"

"It's my concern if you are scaring her. She called me in tears after you left. She's vulnerable you know, and you go storming in there."

"Mr Edwards, if I chose to storm in somewhere you would know about it. As it is, my colleague and I had a pleasant, if somewhat short conversation with her before leaving her to her work."

"You had no right."

Instead of getting caught in an infinite loop of accusations and denials, Saric changed the subject.

"What is your relationship to Mrs Fletcher, Mr Edwards?"

Colin looked a little shocked by the question. "Well, er, she's the star of my show."

"But aren't you the treasurer, Mr Edwards? I can't imagine that the treasurer has much to do with actually staging the show. So how do you know each other so well?"

"We don't really, no, we just go to rehearsals together. As you know, I used to work in professional theatre, so I like to attend rehearsals and add what I can. You know, to give something back."

Out of the corner of his eye, Saric could see Sense Check's real-time reporting output lighting up in a variety of colours. He ignored it; it did not take a logic genius to work out what was going on here.

"You don't know each other well but she called you – an acquaintance who sometimes attends rehearsals – when she was crying in fear because of our visit?"

Colin sat in silence.

"Can you explain that to me, Mr Edwards?"

Saric could almost see Colin's brain working. He was not stupid, but he seemed to be the type of man who liked time to plan what he was going to say, and Saric was asking him to think on his feet.

Saric tried something else. "Mr Edwards, perhaps we should remind ourselves of my interest in you and Mrs Fletcher. I have been engaged to investigate the death of Jane Evans. You have shown up as a person of interest due to you being an important client of the deceased."

Saric was not sure that 'important' was an accurate word, but he thought that making the other man feel so might be helpful.

"All I am trying to do is get to the bottom of her death. If there is anything that would help me move on from you and Mrs Fletcher then my only interest would be to find that out, so that I can pursue other lines of inquiry."

The room went quiet again. Colin was processing. Saric reflected that people generally divided into two groups; those who surround themselves with people who are cleverer than them, in an effort to learn more, and those who surround themselves with people who know less, in an effort to look clever. Colin belonged in the latter group.

"Well, if you must know, Sarah and I are in love."

The way he said it was strange. Not seeing each other, not in a relationship. In love.

Saric nodded. *Silence will be useful here,* he thought.

"It all started when she joined the group two years ago. You wouldn't have recognised her then. She was so shy. But she had talent, I saw that straight away."

Saric nodded encouragingly.

"So, I offered to help her with her part, and we got talking. Her husband is terrible to her. Not violent you understand, but emotionally cruel. He controls where she goes and when. He doesn't even know about the theatre. He thinks she is at a Bible study group. He doesn't believe in the stuff himself, but he's happy for her to go if it keeps her quiet.

"When it came to choosing a show for this year, I pulled a few strings to do this one. It's the perfect part for her and I really wanted her to shine. She wasn't sure, of course, so I spent every Tuesday and Wednesday evening helping her, so that she was well prepared for rehearsals on a Thursday. It's just about giving her confidence, really; it's all there if she would just believe in herself. Anyway, we spent so much time together that one day, while we were rehearsing the scene where she is alone in the forest, I just looked at her and I knew I was in love with her. She feels it too. She won't leave her husband, though, she's too scared of what he might do, but I thought that maybe if she could just be the star this week, she might start to believe what I'm saying, and that might be enough to give her the courage."

He trailed off. Saric felt a wave of sadness. He had never married, but he knew the fulfilment it brought to others, and the pain that it could bring when it went wrong. More importantly, it was a more convincing reason for Colin to have arrived at his door.

"Mr Edwards, thank you for telling me that. I don't believe that we will need to speak to Mrs Fletcher further, so please do thank her for her time and let her know that we won't be bothering her again.

"While you are here, there were just a couple of other points I'd like to check with you. I know you answered some of them on Thursday evening, but I'm afraid my colleague's notes weren't as comprehensive as I'd hoped."

Saric crossed his fingers that Colin would have forgotten the conversation was recorded.

"Ah, yes, my assistant is just the same," Colin agreed, as if pleased for the opportunity to let Saric know he had an assistant.

"On the evening in question, you were at the theatre. Is that correct?"

"Yes, I went to the theatre. In London, where I used to work. They are showing The Full Moon at the moment. It's not bad. I went up on the train from Crawley to Victoria, and jumped on the tube to Piccadilly Circus, walked to the show, watched it and came home the same way."

"Interesting," Saric said idly, "wouldn't it be better to get the tube to Leicester Square?"

"It's closer, yes," agreed Colin, "but it's always so full of tourists who don't know where they are going, so I always use Piccadilly Circus instead."

"What did you think of the play?"

"I thought it was excellent, a novel interpretation with some bold choices that really paid off. If you get a chance you should see it."

"Thank you, Mr Edwards, if I get a chance, I will do that, and thank you for the advice about the stations."

Looking rather pleased with himself, Colin Edwards shook Saric's hand and left.

CHAPTER 27

Jim Callagher was troubled by his encounter with Saric. He had driven home in a daze, his heart racing. He knew that he was furious, but he had stayed on top in this part of the world by taking measured action. He was no less vicious for it, but when he let his rage out, it was always with a purpose.

And there was something else at play here that he could not acknowledge, even to himself, until the following morning; he was scared. Saric knew who he was, and he did not care. He had looked Saric straight in the eye and felt like a victim. Those eyes were dreadful. There was nothing in that man that Jim could get an edge on; no mercy.

Jim weighed it all up in his mind. His boys had taken a beating and word was out. That was certainly unsatisfactory, but the details that had been circulating were vague. As far as he could tell, no one knew who was involved. Retribution would not really achieve much for his reputation. Or at least, the target could really be anyone, and that would be a clear enough message that he was not weakening. But that was only part of the problem. The more concerning element for Jim was having this private detective looking into the affairs of Spencer & Evans. Tony Spencer had been a valuable part of his operation for many years. He knew Tony could not go on forever, and a solution to unpicking his side of the business from his partner's would have been yet another problem, had the troublesome Jane Evans issue not been so neatly resolved. The police had shown no interest in Jim on that front, and he wanted it kept that way. It was easy to keep the rougher elements of his business at arm's length, but the money side was more complicated. After all, in the end he had to get his hands on the money. Keeping Tony out of sight was very important to him.

It was clear that Saric had connections at the police, just as Jim did. This could all get very messy.

Something else did not sit right for Jim; the teaming up of Saric and Rob. When he had been briefed, he had painted an image in his mind of Rob as a worker, maybe hired muscle or general assistant, but he had clearly misjudged that. Were they a couple? *Could be these days*, Jim thought, but social media showed Rob as a married man with one child, a boy. Whatever they were together, the relationship mattered to Saric, and it seemed important to Rob, too.

Rob seemed to have given up on Facebook about five years ago, and they could not find anything online about his wife at all. The boy would be a nice, innocent eight-year-old by now. Jim had an instinct for weak spots in people. It seemed to him Saric only had one: Rob. So, he had an angle, now he needed to be absolutely clear what he wanted. No one else had been in the room at his meeting with Saric; the humiliation was his alone and would never be shared. He thought hard and untangled what he needed from what he would like to see. It was simple really; keep them away from Tony. He would make a statement of authority elsewhere. And he would leave Saric in no doubt over who was in command of the situation, without going straight to an all-out confrontation.

If Saric's weakness was Rob, deciding Rob's weakness was easy; he had a son.

Jim sent one of the men he trusted. An accomplice watched the house until no one had come or go for two hours. It was the middle of the day. The kid should be at school and Mum and Dad presumably at work. There was no need to go creeping around in the dark for this type of break in. They would not need to leave with much.

The second man drove up in a non-descript white van. He got out wearing tradesman's overalls. He looked entirely unremarkable, like a dozen other tradespeople working around the suburban area where Rob lived. He took his time walking up the path to the front door, looking for any signs of someone home, but all was still. He rang the doorbell and when no one answered, as anticipated, he walked round to the back of the house carrying a toolbox. There were no neighbours in the gardens on either side. This was too easy. He took a short crowbar from his toolbox and prized open the back door in one easy motion. Now he was at risk, so he had to move quickly.

He entered a small kitchen. The crockery was piled in the sink. Some of the plates had old food remnants stuck hard to them. A huge bag of pasta was open on the counter, while next to it was an open tub of protein shake and a bunch of bananas. Something was missing, but the intruder let the feeling slide.

He walked through the lounge that flowed into an open-plan dining room. The dining table had been pushed up to the wall to accommodate a weights bench and free weights were all around. The man was looking for something that represented the boy. Some homework pinned to the fridge, or a picture on the mantelpiece. There were pictures, but none with an eight-year-old in them. If there was nothing upstairs, one of these older ones would perhaps do.

At the top of the landing were four doors. The one to the bathroom was ajar but was unlikely to be useful. He opened the first. A double bed at the side of the room had been recently slept in and was unmade. The rest of the room was full of the sort of junk that should have gone up in the loft. There was a fan, an old desktop computer and monitor, a rolled-up rug, boxes of paperwork, and more. Nothing of emotional value was likely to be in there.

The next room was the master bedroom. It was neat and had been decorated with some class. There were his and hers bedside tables and makeup was arranged on top of the chest of drawers. Before investigating in there, he opened the last door, which was the child's bedroom. Ignoring the master bedroom, he entered.

The room was musty and needed a good blast of fresh air. A single bed was in the corner, neatly made with a bright duvet with pictures of diggers and tractors on it. *These bloody people*, the man thought, *ponsing about thinking they are so superior whilst they breed these pathetic bloody kids.*

225

They would not catch his boy going to bed under a digger duvet surrounded by bloody teddy bears at eight years old. A collection of hardback books had been squashed into a bookshelf under the window. The man thought nothing of it. Opposite the bed, a small plastic workbench looked almost new. On the pillow of the bed was a clearly well-loved cuddly dog, neatly placed with the duvet pulled up over its feet. Its long ears had lost their filling.

That will do, he thought, and shoved the toy into his pocket.

He left the room. His instinct was to have a look around for a little bonus, but Jim had said no, and that was that. He left the doors how he found them, walked back downstairs and straight out the back door. The owners would know they had been broken into, and the tension of trying to find out why would add a little drama. That's what Jim had said anyway. The man did not really care. It was just a job, and it could not have been easier. He drove away with the much loved 'Squashy Dog' in his pocket. It was a toy that Rob's father had bought for his first grandson. He had presented it to the boy in the hospital, on the very first day of his life.

CHAPTER 28

DECEMBER 2016

Overall, Martha was happy with Daniel's progress. The thoughts she had been planting had generally stuck well. Sometimes too well. She did not need him expressing any contrary views to anyone but her, and she had found it tricky to moderate her approach to achieve this.

It was not hard to encourage Daniel to focus on Mary as the central figure from whom to take his instruction. The Community believed they had found the true Christianity. In fact, their religion was a confused and incoherent jumble of different branches of Christianity, which had long since lost any true connection to the real teachings of any major Church, but the tradition of Mary, recast as the Great Mother, as a central figure to the faith was consistent with their beliefs.

Her version of Martha had gained general acceptance amongst most of her contemporaries. The Elders were going to take a bit more time to accept her, and some of those more than others. Her parents' focus was quite clearly on their grandchild. The resistance of her early days back in the community had left such a dent in their hopes of having their daughter back that it seemed even the newly formed Martha was too much effort for them. Her son would be much easier to educate. Although it was painful for Martha to accept her parents were lost to her, it did make things easier. She doubted her mother really believed that the Martha she was presenting was the real her, despite how willingly she tried.

Morning prayer was at 10 am. She would go with Daniel. The meeting would start with a short introduction from whoever had been chosen to lead the session that morning, followed by guided prayer. Daniel was leading today's prayers.

As they gathered in the room, a little chat was allowed.

"Are you leading us today?" asked a mild-looking young woman. *She could be pretty*, thought Martha, but she was not.

"Yes, young sister," said Daniel. He smiled at her. He looked confident that he could teach her something.

The room was filling up. Daniel's guests were of mixed ages and there was no disparity between the number of men and women. One Elder was present.

The presence of an Elder in the room would intimidate many prayer leaders, but not Daniel. He was one of a favoured group that the Elders had great confidence in. He clearly anticipated being an Elder himself one day. He had, of course, to pass the test he had been given of bringing Martha back. But that was going well. She was happier spending time with him now, and he always felt so positive after being with her. There was definitely something special about her. It was something he could not quite pin down, but it was a clear feeling that he could not question.

When the room was settled, Daniel began. "Hello, my brothers and sisters."

"Hello, Daniel," the group replied in unison.

"Does anyone in the group have an issue to raise?" Daniel looked around. The dynamic was well established. The Elder would say nothing; if he wanted to raise anything, he would simply take control of the meeting entirely. The youngest members would not speak, for fear of getting something wrong. No one noticeably older than the prayer leader would raise anything either, as they would not wish to look like they were deferring authority to a younger member. All eyes would turn to those in between these groups. And they knew it was up to them.

"I have something I would like to ask for support on."

It was a man of around the same age as Daniel.

"I have found my mind wandering during evening prayer. I have much on my mind with our Christmas celebrations coming."

"I understand; we are all looking forward to our celebrations. It is truly a time for us to focus on the Great Mother, the mother of our saviour, as she brings him into the world. We can find so much comfort from her words."

Martha winced. Maybe she was pushing him too far. That was not the answer they were expecting. She looked at the Elder. He was one of the softer members of the Elder group, and he enjoyed nothing more than a quiet moment in prayer with his fellow members. He had already zoned out of the preamble. Martha was relieved.

The man who raised the question looked a little confused.

"It is becoming increasingly clear to me that it is through the Great Mother that we will find the truth."

Others in the room looked puzzled.

"The Great Mother is talking to me," Daniel began.

"She—" interrupted Martha, trying not to sound desperate "—she talks to us all, doesn't she? It seems to me right to remember the Great Mother at this time, as the mother of Our Lord on earth. I wonder if you should talk about Jesus at this time too?"

"Quite so, Martha, and thank you. Let's talk about Jesus at the time of the upcoming nativity."

He was back on track.

No harm done, thought Martha. She would have to work on keeping Daniel's evolving fascination with the Great Mother just between them.

CHAPTER 29

After Colin left his office, Saric sat in silence for a long time. Something did not make sense. Murder was often a complex crime to unpick, but it was also simple. When you took away the circumstances in which the victim was found, and the evidence and the mechanics of how it was done, what it required more than anything else was a motive.

Saric believed that anyone was capable of murder, if the motive was there, but for most people that would have to be something compelling. Normal people did not just wake up one morning and decide to take another person's life. There had to be a reason.

For someone like Jim, that reason might be the threat to his business or his reputation. These things were important to him, and there were enough rumours that he had arranged other deaths that Saric was confident he was capable of it.

Phillip was more complicated. He was unhappy certainly, but that unhappiness was the slow, creeping kind. Not a fiery anger. And Phillip was not Jim. Murder would be new to him. Would the slow build-up of resentment towards his wife be enough to provoke Phillip to force a pillow over the face of a person he had spent fifteen years with?

And then there was Colin. There was nothing about the man that was remarkable. Although he job title was Financial Controller, he was really just another accountant, following a path that had been laid out for him since birth, if unsuccessfully. If it were not for Sense Check, Saric would discount Colin right now, but there were so many flags from the interviews that he couldn't ignore. Even if all he did was explain them in order to eliminate him, he had to look further.

He reviewed the output Sense Check had produced following Colin's visit. The most useful was a transcript of the conversation that started when they entered the study.

Saric: "Mr Edwards *[GREEN – my colleague and I met with Mrs Fletcher at her office yesterday],* because there were a couple of points we wanted to clarify with her. We did not invade her office, we spoke for about five minutes before leaving. *[GREEN – Two of her colleagues were present for the whole conversation.]*"

Sense Check had highlighted Saric's words in green where it had matched them against external references. In this case, Saric's diary for two days previously. It was a limitation that Sense Check had cross referenced a statement made by Saric against a source he had produced. This would be a problem if the same logic were applied to a statement from a suspect, but as Saric was confident he was not relevant to this case, he made a note to arrange for that area of the code to be looked at and moved on.

Colin: "[BLUE – She has nothing to do with this.]"

Blue text meant a statement for which Sense Check did not have enough evidence. Saric chose to ignore this flag; while it was true that they could not rule out that Sarah was involved, he thought there were better areas to focus on. Sense Check was excellent at applying logic but much less useful in prioritising which illogical conclusions mattered.

Saric: "We did not suggest that she did, we were just interested in her view of things."

Colin: "What things?"

Saric: "That is not really your concern, Mr Edwards"

Colin: "[BLUE – It's my concern if you are scaring her. She called me in tears after you left. She's vulnerable, you know, and you go storming in there.]"

Saric: "Mr Edwards, if I chose to storm in somewhere you would know about it. As it is, my colleague and I had a pleasant, if somewhat short conversation with her before leaving her to her work."

Colin: "You had no right."

Saric: "What is your relationship to Mrs Fletcher, Mr Edwards?"

Colin: "Well, er, [BLUE – she's the star of my show.]"

Saric: "But aren't you the treasurer, Mr Edwards? I can't imagine that the treasurer has much to do with actually staging the show. So how do you know each other so well?"

Colin: "[BLUE – We don't really, no, we just go to rehearsals together.] [GREEN – I used to work in professional theatre] as you know, so [BLUE – I like to attend rehearsals and add what I can.] You know, to give something back."

Saric: "You don't know each other well but she called you – an acquaintance who sometimes attends rehearsals – when she was crying in fear because of our visit?"

Saric: "Can you explain that to me, Mr Edwards?"

Saric: "Mr Edwards, perhaps we should remind ourselves of my interest in you and Mrs Fletcher. [GREEN – I have been engaged to investigate the death of Jane Evans. You have shown up as a person of interest due to you being an important client of the deceased.] All I am trying to do is get to the bottom of her death. If there is anything that would help me move on from you and Mrs Fletcher then my only interest would be to find that out so that I can pursue other lines of inquiry."

Colin: "Well, if you must know, [BLUE – Sarah and I are in love.]"

Colin: "[YELLOW – It all started when she joined the group two years ago.] [BLUE – You wouldn't have recognised her then. She was so shy. But she had talent, I saw that straight away.]"

Yellow. A statement that could be tested to strengthen a conclusion. Saric was unsure why Sense Check was so keen to validate Sarah, and then reminded himself that it was not keen to do anything at all. Either way, Sarah's membership of the group would be easy to validate but ultimately insignificant.

Colin: "So I offered to help her with her part and we got talking. [BLUE

– Her husband is terrible to her. Not violent you understand, but emotionally cruel. He controls where she goes and when. He doesn't even know about the theatre. He thinks she is at a Bible study group. He doesn't believe in the stuff himself, but he's happy for her to go if it keeps her quiet.]

When it came to choosing a show for this year, [BLUE – I pulled a few strings to do this one]. It's the perfect part for her and I really wanted her to shine. She wasn't sure, of course, so I spent [YELLOW – every Tuesday and Wednesday evening helping her] so she was well prepared for rehearsals on a Thursday. It's just about giving her confidence, really; it's all there if she would just believe in herself. Anyway, we spent so much time together that one day, while we were rehearsing the scene where she is alone in the forest, I just looked at her and knew I was in love with her. [BLUE – She feels it too. She won't leave her husband, though], she's too scared of what he might do, but I thought that maybe if she could just be the star this week, she might start to believe what I'm saying, and that might be enough to give her the courage."

This was more interesting. Jane had been murdered on a Tuesday. Colin's alibi was that he was at the theatre on a Wednesday, so this statement could not in fact be true. In reality, Saric knew that Colin was probably using the description "every Tuesday and Wednesday" with an invisible caveat of "unless there was an exception", but it was still a point to check.

Saric: "Mr Edwards, thank you for telling me that. [BLUE – I don't believe that we will need to speak to Mrs Fletcher further], so please do thank her for her time and let her know that we won't be bothering her again.

While you are here, there were just a couple of other points I'd like to check with you. I know you answered some of them on Thursday evening, but [RED – I'm afraid my colleague's notes weren't as comprehensive as I'd hoped.]"

Sense Check NOTE 1: Sense Check transcript Thursday 25th June and field notes available, appear complete.

Saric could not help but chuckle as he was caught out in his own lie. Of course, Rob's notes were complete and correct and supported by Sense Check's own transcription of the meeting, but he was glad that the software didn't let him off the hook.

Where an obvious lie was identified, Sense Check added a note to explain how it had reached the conclusion, and Saric enjoyed the way the machine appeared to be defending its own work on this one.

Colin: "Ah, yes, my assistant is just the same."

Saric: "On the evening in question you were at the theatre, is that correct?"

Colin: "Yes, "[BLUE – I went to the theatre. In London.] [GREEN – Where I used to work. They are showing The Full Moon at the moment.] It's not bad. [YELLOW – I went up on the train from Crawley to Victoria, and jumped on the tube to Piccadilly Circus, walked to the show, watched it and] [RED – came home the same way.]"

A whole rainbow of conclusions here reminded Saric that they had no external verification of Colin's alibi or that he was even known in the theatre world, as he claimed to be. In fact, they had not yet verified his journey. The yellow indicated that the description was too vague for Sense Check to validate the statement from the travel data available to it. For that it would need to know which trains Colin took. This required follow up, but what interested Saric was the red phrase at the end.

Sense Check NOTE 2: Conflicts with Transport for London information on station closures.

He clicked a link that took him to a website listing travel data for the whole of London on the evening of 16th June. He scrolled down until he reached the point he wanted. Piccadilly Circus Underground Station was closed from 6.48 pm that evening until 4.00 am the next morning, due to a 'passenger incident'.

Sense Check NOTE 3: Text match to interview of 25th June – a hundred per cent

Curious. The words Colin had used to describe his journey were exactly the same as the words he had used at the theatre, which Sense Check had also transcribed. When people were telling the truth, their memory would generally project the events slightly differently, depending on the context of the conversation, and this would usually result in recalling the same events differently. So, the facts would stay the same, but the words might change. This seemed more like a script, a line that Colin had prepared and rehearsed to give when asked. It was not the first time Saric had seen Colin prepare words. He had done the same on stage and at the front door. But even innocent people began to panic when asked to give an alibi, so it might be nothing.

Saric: "Interesting, wouldn't it be better to get the tube to Leicester Square?"

Colin: "[GREEN – It's closer], yes, but it's always so full of tourists who don't know where they are going, so [RED – I always use Piccadilly Circus instead.]"

Sense Check NOTE 4: Conflicts with Transport for London information on station closures.

Colin was certain of this statement, which could not possibly be true. If he was describing a journey he took a lot, it would probably be easy enough for him to forget that the station was closed, but surely he would have remembered when prompted that he had taken an alternative route.

Saric: "What did you think of the play?"

Colin: "[RED – I thought it was excellent, a novel interpretation with some bold choices that really paid off. If you get a chance you should see it.]"

Sense Check NOTE 5: Conflicts with earlier assertion.

Sense Check NOTE 6: Cross reference to www.theatrereviews.co.uk/fullmoon

Sense Check objected to this statement in two ways. Clicking on the links, Saric could see that the program had identified that the statement conflicted with Colin's earlier assertion that the play was "not bad", and also that the description he had given was a ninety-six per cent match for the wording in an online review. It wasn't impossible that this was a coincidence, of course, but it was an interesting observation.

Saric: "Thank you, Mr Edwards, if I get a chance, I will do that, and thank you for the advice about the stations."

Saric sat back in his deep leather chair and sighed. He wished he could eliminate any one of these suspects, but at the moment he felt no further on than he had done three days ago. Each of these men were hiding things, but it was not yet possible to tell which one of them might be hiding a murder.

CHAPTER 30

It had been a long day at the office for Rob, who was thinking only of getting home to have a couple of beers before falling into bed. He pulled his car into the gravel drive and turned off the engine. He sat for a few moments appreciating the silence and the space. Then he pulled himself out of the car and ambled up the narrow path that led to the front door. It was still spring, but it had been dry, and the overgrown plants that lined the path were turning brown at the edges. He felt a wave of guilt that he was not tending the garden how he should and resolved that tomorrow would be the day that he got around to it.

He turned the key in the door and stepped into the hall. Even before it was fully shut, he knew something was wrong. Something in the way the air moved around the familiar space was not right, or maybe it was the way the light was spreading across the walls. He stepped into the kitchen and found that the old stable door was open. For a moment, he wondered if he had left it ajar, but before that thought had even left his mind, he knew this was not the case – he had not set foot in the garden for weeks. No, someone had been here.

He ran back through the house and took the stairs two at a time, adrenaline rising with every step. Without slowing, he burst through the final door on the landing and into his son's room. He knew this image exactly, where every item sat, and every item lay untouched except one. Two parts of Rob's mind battled each other. One part wanted to drop to the floor and disappear; it held him frozen to the spot and he could not think. But the other part of his mind wanted action. Without conscious instruction, he fished his phone out of his pocket and called Saric.

Saric answered on the first ring. "What's wrong?"

It was like he knew.

"Someone's been here" were the only words that came out.

"Are you OK?"

Silence.

"Rob, are you safe? . . . Rob?"

Somehow, he formed the words. "I'm fine. They're not here. They've got Squashy Dog."

Rob wasn't sure what happened next or how long Saric took to arrive, but soon he was sitting in the leather armchair with a large scotch in his hand. Saric was sitting across from him.

"Rob, I've had a look around and I can't see that anything else was taken. All the valuables are still here. It looks like they came and left through the back door."

It sounded to Rob like Saric was a long way away, as if there was a delay between the words leaving his mouth and reaching his brain.

"We have to find him, Saric."

Saric gave him a look that Rob did not understand. "I'll deal with it," he said with determination, like this was not a matter for Rob to argue with.

This did not make sense. They should be calling the police to investigate, to look for fingerprints and to follow-up leads. Or Saric should be promising to find whoever did this. "I'll deal with this" was not right. He looked again. The look on Saric's face was guilt.

"What's going on?"

"Rob, I'll deal with this. This is my fault. I misjudged something and it's my responsibility to resolve it."

"You misjudged? What does that mean?" The words were louder than he meant them to be. "Someone has come into my house and taken one of the only things in my life that matters, and you talk of misjudging it? Tell me what's going on."

Saric was silent for a long time, weighing up whether to explain. The guilt on his face was mixed with something else now. *Sadness*, Rob thought, *and compassion*.

"Rob, I'm sorry. Like I said, this is my fault. I know what that toy meant to you. Three days ago, I had a visit from Jim Callagher. He wasn't happy that we made him look incompetent when we defended ourselves against his men. He also wasn't happy that we were looking at him for the Jane Evans case. I thought we had reached an understanding, but I was wrong."

"Why didn't you tell me? That was days ago."

"You were dealing with a lot, worried about Sarah. I didn't think you needed to know at that stage. Believe me when I say he will pay for this, but we need to deal with this in the right way. We still have him in the frame for Jane Evans and we can't let this escalate into an all-out war."

"That dog is his favourite toy."

Always in the present tense, Saric noted. "I know, I will find him," he promised, wondering which 'him' he was referring to.

CHAPTER 31

Rob and Saric arrived at Phillip's house in the early afternoon. Phillip had called Rob early that morning having been released by the police, who, despite what Deputy Chief Stephens had said, didn't have enough evidence to charge him with Jane Evans's murder. Phillip wanted an update on the case and demanded that Rob and Saric meet with him immediately. Saric had been working on something else that morning and refused to meet until he had finished, but Rob had persuaded him to compromise and they agreed they would visit Phillip at home that afternoon. Saric could sometimes get so occupied on a secret project that nothing else could happen until it was resolved, and Rob knew better than to try and force him.

The Evans' house was a large, detached property on a small but prestigious commuter estate on the outskirts of town, where, at the weekends, rows of BMWs would sit gleaming on large drives outside a series of identical properties. At this time on a weekday, though, almost all of the residents were at work, so the only presence on the estate was a series of cars belonging to the cleaners and gardeners. Neither Rob nor

Saric would choose to live in this kind of place. For Saric, it was neither close enough to town to feel connected to the rest of the world nor remote enough to feel away from it. For Rob it simply lacked soul.

The man who answered the bright red door was barely recognisable as the same man who had marched into their office just a week earlier. He looked exhausted; his previously well-kept beard had grown out and he had large dark circles under each eye. His expensive suit had gone, and he looked to be wearing yesterday's clothes. Rob knew better than to think there was any one right way to deal with grief – he had plenty of first-hand experience to understand that – but he thought the way Phillip looked right now was somewhere closer to what he had expected when he first met the recently bereaved man.

Phillip had lost none of his confidence, however, and spent the first few minutes of the meeting berating the men for their lack of progress.

"I engaged you because I was told you get results, but I've seen nothing. The police still think it was me and even my lawyers struggled to get them to release me – and they really are the best, you should see what they charge!"

Rob let Phillip rant. He needed it. Saric sat motionless. As Phillip slowly ran out of steam, Rob started the meeting again. They had agreed in the car on the way to the house that it was still possible that Phillip had murdered Jane, and so there was a careful balance to strike between keeping their client up to date with progress and telling a potential murderer details of innocent people. They had decided that Rob should lead the meeting and keep it as vague as possible, whilst still making Phillip feel like they were on his side.

"Since we last spoke, we have been following a number of leads and have identified several people of interest from both Jane's professional and personal life. We have interviewed four individuals and consulted with experts in various areas of accountancy and forensics."

"But have you found him yet?"

"Not yet. There are still a number of areas where we need to gather more information, but we do think the areas we are looking at will lead to answers."

"I need more than that." Phillip looked desperate. "Who are you looking at for this?"

"I'm not sure it would be appropriate for us to disclose that to you at this stage, Phillip."

"Because you think I did it?"

Rob looked at the man sat across from him. A week ago, his wiry frame had looked athletic. Today, he looked weak, broken. The phone by Phillip's side beeped with a message not a call. He glanced over at it but didn't pick it up. "Phillip, if I tell you who we are talking to, what would you do with the information?"

Anger flashed across the other man's face. "I'd find him and I'd . . ." he trailed off. "OK, I take your point, but promise me you will find him."

"We are doing our best, Phillip, we have many promising leads . . ." Rob started the standard explanation he had rehearsed for when victims asked him to do this. Never promise what you can't deliver. He knew that even the best investigators can't solve every crime. A breath caught at the back of his lungs. He looked up and faced Phillip, who seemed to dissolve even further.

"I did love her, you know."

This statement took Rob by surprise, but if Phillip noticed, he didn't allow it to interrupt his flow.

"I know it must seem like I didn't, and I know I haven't behaved well towards her, but we were happy together. We met at a mutual friend's wedding. Did I tell you that? We were so young then, but she was so vibrant, had such ambition. I know people think accountants are boring, but she never was. We used to travel all over the world, you know. That photo over there was taken while we were travelling around South East Asia. We spent a whole summer there and it was taken on our last night before we came back to the UK. That was seventeen years ago."

Rob looked at the photo. It was a black and white image of two young people on a beach, drinking cocktails in front of the sunset. They both had huge smiles on their faces, a whole life ahead of them full of promise. Phillip's phone beeped again. Reflex made him pick it up and look at the screen. He put it back on the coffee table.

"Sorry," Phillip said, "she doesn't understand."

So that must be the woman from the office, Rob realised.

"She thinks that this changes things. It does, but not in the way she thinks it should. It was a mistake. I was stupid to think anything else. I'm only glad that Jane never knew for sure."

"The police think you killed Jane so that you could be with your new girlfriend."

Sometimes, Saric sat so quietly in a room that you could forget he was there until he spoke. For a moment, Phillip looked shocked, like he might react against this, but then he sank back into his chair.

"I know they do, and I can see why. The texts between me and Jane that day were horrible, and I wish I'd never sent them, but I didn't mean what I said any more than she did. And now Holly won't leave me alone."

He nodded at the phone. "The picture she paints is that I was about to leave Jane to be with her, and that's what the police have chosen to believe. But that isn't how any of this was. I never promised her that, and if she chose to believe it then that's not my fault, is it? It was just nice to feel wanted, and to be honest, I was quite flattered by the attention. Of course, I know she was only interested in my money, but she is much younger than me and, well, it made a change from the constant bickering at home. But for the police to think that I could ever kill Jane is mad. They are saying that Holly had a criminal record. Apparently, she had a drug problem, but she conveniently never mentioned that. They say her last boyfriend was a local dealer. I knew nothing about any of it."

"That's interesting, Phillip, did they say why this was relevant to the case?"

"The police say Jane was injected with drugs before she was suffocated. There was a puncture wound and drugs in her system."

Phillip looked stricken as he said the words out loud, as if acknowledging for the first time that this was real.

*

As they drove back to the office, Rob and Saric discussed Phillip and what the new information added to the case.

"I'd like to get the transcript into Sense Check, and the drugs angle is interesting, but I'm not sure we learned anything new about him."

Saric was still brooding over being summoned by Phillip.

"I'm not sure that's true," said Rob. Sometimes, he forgot that his friend had a more limited view of what things could be learned in such a meeting. "I think we learned a lot."

"Such as?"

"Well, I believed him when he said he loved his wife and that he wasn't planning to leave her for this Holly. The way he looked, Saric, you can't fake that. And if he wasn't trying to leave her then where is his motive?"

"There are no facts in what you said. That's just opinion. You can't prove that one person loves another, even though there are some interesting advances in brain imaging that may prove helpful in such matters in future."

"You can't prove it," conceded Rob, "but that doesn't mean it isn't true."

CHAPTER 32

MAY 2017

Martha and Daniel were sitting on a bench looking over the lake. The sun was high and reflected off the water. It was hot. Initially, Martha had found it a little awkward to adjust to applying a hypnotic mood to these conditions. She had always ensured the environment for her clients presented the minimum amount of potential disruption. Low lighting, comfortably warm, minimal background noise; the whole thing was set up to feel like somewhere a client would expect to be hypnotised. Out here was different. She had to be able to take the opportunities when they came. Whenever she and Daniel were alone, she would work on him.

It had been over a year since she had first introduced to Daniel the notion that she was something special. She had taken her inspiration from a documentary she watched when she was studying. It was all about miracles, and she remembered being mystified by the visitings of Mary, Jesus's mother, to girls in faraway rural towns in Europe; towns that have since become renowned places of worship. She had always wondered whether the same effect could be achieved with hypnosis, and even whether that was exactly how it was done. Or else they just lied to themselves until they believed it. Or perhaps, in distressing moments of profound confusion, she wondered if they really were miracles; miracles she could never understand. Whatever it was, she was determined that Daniel was going to believe she was the Great Mother's mouthpiece on earth, and that only he could learn the truth until the time came for the enlightening, at which point he would be raised up so that all would learn from him.

In common with most therapists, Martha had developed a particular faith in some techniques more than others. Rationally, she knew this was an unhelpful bias, probably driven by her own reaction to others using these approaches on her, but nevertheless, she could not help but put some higher up the scale of impact than others.

Now was the time to apply one of her favourites.

She could see that Daniel was comfortable. They had plenty of time, and she had taught him the value of spending moments of silence with her, which she would use to gently mirror his movements at first, before taking the lead. Once she had him following her, she would edge him into a comfortable position. Then she followed his breathing pattern and prepared to match the rhythm to the timbre of her voice.

"Daniel," she said, "it's lovely out here today."

"Yes, it is."

"You know, I've been starting to *relax more and more as you sit here* with me. I think it's maybe in the way the sun seems to reach down and warm me with its soothing glow, as if *all your muscles are getting softer and softer*."

Daniel had become accustomed to listening to Martha's soft voice at times like this, and he always felt so calm and reassured afterwards that he had stopped questioning what was going on.

"I am so comfortable when I am with you, Martha," he said. "You truly have the Great Lord in your spirit."

"Yes," she said, "and look at the miracle before you, Daniel. The glorious sunshine settling on the water. Look how the water ripples out and out; it makes me think of the way it feels to *let your mind wander* to the places where the Great Lord reaches out to us. And as you *look at the water*, you can start to *imagine how it would feel to be able to hear the truth being given directly to you now*, so that it doesn't matter whether you keep your eyes open or let them gently shut. Either way, you know that you are ready to hear the truth."

Daniel closed his eyes. She had him.

"Now, to hear the truth, you need to let your mind wander. If you wanted to see the whole of your life laid out before you, let's wonder, would it be a line in front of you, or within you, or something else? Which is it for you?"

"It's in front of me."

"And if the future was at one end and the past at the other, would the past be on the left?"

"Yes."

"And if you wanted to be above that line, would it be easier for you to move above it, or for the line to move below you?"

"Move above it."

"That's right. And if you wanted to move along the line, would it be easier for you or the line to move?"

"Me to move."

"That's perfect. So, move along the line now until you can see yourself looking down. Notice all the things that let you know how calm and relaxed you feel."

She watched his face intently, and once happy he was there, she continued. "As you look down at yourself now, it could be interesting to notice the things about you that let you know you have become the channel for the Great Mother; how she is with you now, how you have always known it would be you, because you are the one she has chosen. As you see the spirit around you, start to notice the deep sense of inner peace and knowing that makes you aware that you are the chosen one, and that only I am talking to you, and you can hear my voice. You understand this. *My voice is* in *the spirit* that you know is the place of certainty."

She paused to allow his mind to cycle through that thought for a moment and let it develop. "Now, taking your time, allow yourself to move back a long time, over your line and into the past, to the first time you remember that feeling of certainty, of spirit, of knowing the great joy and peace of *the Great Mother is with you*."

His mind, now open to search for such an enticing moment, slipped over the deliberately messy grammar that allowed Martha to build the image the way she wanted. Again, she followed his face and body carefully until she was happy he was there.

"As you look down on that image, it would be interesting to allow all of your senses to be filled with the sensation of inner peace, total certainty and calm. Feeling the very first time the truth came to you completely. And we can wonder what it is in that image that lets you know I am there. It could be something you can see, hear or feel, or something else; and that just lets you know that everything you have ever known about the truth has come from this voice. It has always been me. *Everything that you know to be true in your life has been from me*."

She paused again. She could see in his body language that this was not being resisted, so she carried on. "When you are ready to learn everything you need to know from this younger you, move down into his body and feel what it feels like to have that knowledge. Take it all in, through whatever senses allow you to experience that first moment of total truth, knowing more and more with each breath how the truth was revealed to you through me. And when you are ready to leave that point, taking with you all you need to, move back above the line so you are looking down on your younger self once more."

When he was ready, she continued. "As you move back towards today, it could be interesting to notice all the things that have happened in your life over the years that have allowed you to recognise the truth in what has been revealed to you. It might be straight away, or it might be later that you start to realise the impact of my truth, which has always been there throughout your life, as you move closer and closer to now, noticing the time I chose to reveal myself to you again in person, the way we are today. And it all means that you are ready to hear the truth. So that as you return to today, and feel the warm sun on your body, all over your body you will experience the full truth about who you are, who I am, and how that means *you are ready to be guided in all your decisions towards the certainty that I give you*." She paused again. Daniel looked perfectly serene. There was not a hint of confusion in his mind.

Martha went on to take Daniel on a soothing journey in his mind to places of calm and quiet, making sure that she left a post-hypnotic layer that would prevent him from wanting to talk about this straight away, and allowing him to come back to the here and now feeling energised and positive and ready to use everything he had learned in the best possible way.

The best possible way for me, Martha thought.

Before she finally encouraged him to open his eyes, she moved between him and the direction of the sun. As he came to, he looked up and saw the silhouette of an angel, her face shaded by the brilliant sunlight radiating all around her. He knew exactly what he was looking at.

His saviour.

Somehow, he had always known.

CHAPTER 33

"I feel like we are chasing ourselves in circles."

Rob was staring out of the car window, as they drove back from the suburbs. "We have suspects, but we are neither proving they did it nor eliminating them."

Rob felt a responsibility towards clients; they came to Saric, and by extension to him, when they needed answers and, regardless of his feelings towards Phillip, at this stage he felt like he was failing his client.

"I think we are further along than you think." Saric did not take his eyes off the road.

"How? What are you thinking?"

"I think we should take a trip to London."

As they drove back towards town, Saric explained the output from Sense Check and the discrepancies in Colin's explanation of where he was on the night of the murder. "I'd like to follow his route to the theatre and back and speak with the staff there. I'd feel better if we had some external verification of his story. If nothing else, at least we might eliminate him. Being at the theatre is a solid alibi, if we can find some witnesses."

It was late afternoon now, and Rob's mind was on the cold beer that was sitting in the fridge at the cottage. "It's getting late, shall we do that tomorrow?"

"Better to do it tonight, then we will be doing the journey at the right time, and there's more chance of catching the theatre staff on duty. That would be easier than having to find a way to contact them at home."

Reluctantly, Rob agreed, and the men drove towards Crawley, where Colin had started his journey. The rush hour traffic was heavy, but as it was heading out of town, their journey was not slowed too much and they managed to find a space in the station car park. They bought tickets and waited on the grey platform for the 5.29 pm train towards London Victoria.

The train was delayed by a few minutes and Rob watched the people waiting on the platform with them. Most of them were commuters leaving the offices and shops around the station. The southbound platform was much busier than the platform on which they stood.

People tended not to commute home out of Crawley towards London.

There was a time when Rob would have stood amongst them, at a different station but with the same expression, boredom twinned with the anticipation of getting home to his family. He did not appreciate then what a joy that was, and now it hurt more than ever.

They found seats in the third carriage of the train. Saric preferred to sit in the seats at the very end of the carriage. Despite having known the man for five years, Rob knew very little about Saric's past, and infinitely less than Saric knew about his, but the fact that he had a preferred seating position on a train reminded Rob that Saric's history included types of strategic training he would rather not know about.

The train was slow and stopped at a long series of stations. As the landscape around them changed from green countryside to grey suburbia, Saric received a call from his contact at the lab. As expected, he had to bargain hard to get the information, which was awkward in the crowded confines of an evening commuter train. Several passengers gave Rob angry looks, as Saric explained what he needed without any concession to the quiet that permeated the carriage by mutual, exhausted consent.

Eventually, Saric conceded that when he received this information it would repay the last of the favours owed from a small matter he had assisted with involving the technician's teenage daughter. This was not strictly true in terms of hours owed, but Saric chose to let it slip in the interests of getting an answer.

As Saric hung up the call, Rob gave him a quizzical glance.

"He's going to get back to us," Saric murmured.

As they left the train at Victoria, they pushed their way through crowds of people waiting impatiently behind the barriers for announcements about platforms and emerged into the large station concourse.

They made their way down a series of stairs to the underground platforms, before using their travelcards to join the Victoria Line heading north. After just one stop, they left the train carriage and swapped lines, before travelling another stop to Piccadilly Circus. At both stations, the platforms were so busy that two trains came and went before they were able to join them. This was all added to the time calculations that would determine whether Colin could have travelled in this way on the night of the murder. Rob found the journey strange. It would have taken no longer to walk to the theatre from Victoria, and a stroll through the park on a warm evening would have been far more pleasant than being pressed against strangers in the stifling heat of a tube carriage. He thought about Colin. He was not a man who expended energy unnecessarily, so the tube made sense.

They arrived at Piccadilly Circus just after 6.30 pm. This was too early to head straight to the theatre. Colin had not mentioned any delays in his journey, which raised a question about what he had done for the next hour. They could check that with him later.

As they had an hour to spare, Rob and Saric found a pub a few doors down from the theatre, where they could pass the time. It was the kind of establishment that seemed out of place in the busy London streets, being an old-fashioned pub, full of dark wood and stonework. Saric brought their drinks and they settled at a small round table in the corner of the room, where they could see the comings and goings at the bar. They spent some time reflecting on the journey they had just completed, but nothing had arisen that either corroborated or refuted Colin's story.

"I've asked Grace to take another look at the stuff we got from Jane's computer, focusing in particular on Colin."

"Why him? Tony and Jim were the dodgy ones, weren't they?" Rob asked.

It was now hard for him to separate his feelings for Jim from the rest of the case. If they could prove it was him then they could see him punished.

"We've exhausted that one. If the combined power of Grace and Sense Check can't find anything in that data, then I'm not sure there can be anything there to find. I doubt they will discover much around Colin, either, but at least it's something to keep us moving."

Saric wanted to take Rob's mind off things. He was not gifted at small talk, having never really been taught it as a child, but of all the people he had met over the years, Rob was the easiest to talk to. Still, he had to pick his subjects carefully. He could not talk about the future, there was only one discussion about the future they could ever have. And Saric had no interest in cars, or sports, or good-looking women off the television, which seemed to be the mainstay of pub-based male conversation. Whilst he could approximate a conversation in any of those areas for professional reasons, Rob knew it was fabricated and would tell Saric so.

They did, however, share a deep interest in anything of a philosophical nature, anything that allowed them to take opposing views and see who could get on top. The arts were a good place to start, especially anything that was trying to make a point. They could argue over what it was supposed to mean and whether the point was well made, or simply whether it was any good, and then what good means. After a few glasses of wine, they could go on for hours.

"What do you make of this amateur dramatics stuff, then?" asked Saric.

"What do you mean? Do you mean, is it necessarily awful and just an unfortunate learning place that proper actors have to graduate from; or is it the life blood of the art form, connecting local people to the theatre?"

"Yes, that."

"Which one?"

"Both. I mean, what's the bloody point of the whole thing? Does anyone ever buy a ticket for amateur dramatics if they don't know one of the cast?"

"Does that matter?" said Rob.

"It matters if you want to know what the point of it is. Is it just a training ground for real art, or is it art itself?"

"I see," said Rob. He took a long drink of his beer to buy some time to think of an answer. "It's art. Just badly performed."

"If I pick up the *Great Gatsby* and read a paragraph out loud to you, is that art?"

"In your weird accent. Definitely not art."

"Would it be art if Patrick Stewart read it out?" asked Saric.

"Suppose not," said Rob. "It's not your fault; it's not art to read a paragraph of a book out loud."

"Why not?"

"Because the art was already formed in the writing of the book, not in the reading it out," said Rob.

"But in theatre, the art is not the script, it is the performance," said Saric.

271

"I agree, it is the performance that makes it art, even if the performance is poor. You're agreeing with me," said Rob.

"Surely, it's relative, though? If you watch a bunch of five-year-old kids doing a nativity, you can't argue that's art, can you?" said Saric.

For an uncomfortable moment, Saric realised where he had taken the conversation. He considered moving on quickly, but Rob saved him by sticking on the subject. "You and your relativity argument! Is there nothing you can't hedge? Yes, OK, I'll give you that. There are some performances that are not art and, therefore, are nothing more than practice for the real thing. But if we're going to agree that, we're going to have to agree that theatre is never art, or that there is no art at all."

"Why?" Saric looked a little disappointed at the idea of disproving the existence of art.

"If you put all theatre performances on a non-art to art spectrum, you have a graduated scale, with a binary decision embedded. In other words, you are going to have to pick a single performance in the history of all performances that tips non-art to art. And that's absurd."

"Fair point," admitted Saric.

"Maybe the real question is not whether it is or isn't art, but whether it is or isn't any good," said Rob.

"Well, maybe," said Saric. He noticed they'd both nearly finished their beers and knew Rob was about to set off for their second. "But you're going to have to work harder than that to convince me the drivel our man Colin put on, and you made me sit through, is anywhere close to being art!"

At 7.15 pm, they walked to the theatre. Excited patrons were still queuing to get in and mingling at the bar. They watched them as they waited. Tickets were checked by two members of staff at the door. They scanned a barcode on each ticket before letting people through to the foyer, where they either went up various staircases and through different doors to their seats or joined further queues to check coats in the cloakroom, get drinks or buy programmes. A few people stepped back outside to smoke, forming disjointed groups along the pavement, desperate for one last hit of nicotine before the show started. By 7.25 pm, the foyer was almost empty and only a few late comers rushed to get in before the auditorium doors closed. At 7.30 pm, silence fell in the foyer and the front-of-house staff took a break before beginning to prepare for the interval.

273

The box office remained open and Saric asked the attendant if they could see an old colleague of Colin's whom he had mentioned in passing still worked at the theatre. He made an excuse about having a mutual friend, but in reality, people tended to avoid saying no to Saric.

A short time later, a woman in her mid-fifties approached them. She was dressed in the theatre's uniform of a deep red blazer and black trousers, and her dark hair was neatly styled, although a thin strip of grey at the roots proved that this was not its natural colour. She wore more makeup than was needed, which gave her the appearance of someone trying to remain young, which made her look older than she was.

"Hello, I'm Jenny, I understand you want to see me?" She flashed the same fake smile that anyone working in the service industry learns to master, pretending that she did not mind at all that her break had been interrupted.

"Jenny, it's lovely to meet you," said Rob.

Charming older women was one of the areas of the business that Saric generally left to his partner.

"I understand that you are a friend of Colin Edwards. It was actually him who recommended we see the play. We are in town for the next few days and wanted to see if there are any tickets available. We thought that as you know Colin, you might be able to help us."

"Of course." The charm was working, the smile a little more natural. "They can help you with that at the box office. I think there are some available for tomorrow night, or the matinee on Wednesday."

"Thank you. Colin saw the play last week, I think. Did he manage to say hello?"

"Yes, he was here last Tuesday. Actually, have you spoken to him since then?"

"Yes, at the weekend, that's when he mentioned this."

"Oh, that's good. I was actually a bit worried."

"Why's that?" Rob was intrigued now and could tell that Saric was suddenly paying attention.

"Well, I saw him before the show, but I was busy. It's like that here. Incredibly hectic for short bursts and then really quiet. Anyway, we agreed to meet at the bar down the road after the play, when I'd finished work, and get a drink. We haven't seen each other since he worked here, and it would have been nice to catch up. I waited for him for over an hour, but he didn't turn up. Obviously, he was in the theatre most of the night, so nothing could have happened to him, but it was still a bit odd. I was looking forward to seeing him."

"And you are sure this was Tuesday?"

"Yes, absolutely. I don't work on a Wednesday, which is why I didn't mind meeting Colin. Otherwise, by the time I finish work, it's a bit late for socialising when there's an early start the next day."

"He seemed fine at the weekend. We were at his theatre group's performance. Maybe he was worried about that."

Rob felt this was the kindest explanation he could offer for Colin standing her up.

"Yes, that'll be it. Well, if you would like some tickets, I'll show you to the box office."

Rob bought two tickets for a show he had no intention of attending the next night, before they left the theatre.

While they waited for the performance to end, they had dinner in one of the many restaurants that filled this part of London. Most of them were aimed squarely at the thousands of tourists who visited every day. Saric refused to eat in any of them, declaring that the food was overpriced, boring and rushed. Rob tended to agree with him, but he felt much less strongly about the matter. Instead, Saric led him down a narrow side street, where a tapas restaurant occupied the ground floor and basement of a small property. Another of Saric's contacts owned the place and, after greeting them both warmly, she found them a table. Instead of giving them menus, she brought them a series of her favourite dishes, along with an excellent bottle of red.

Rob could have spent hours in this place, chatting idly and setting the world to rights, but by 10 pm, and midway through an argument about whether books could successfully be adapted into plays, it was time to head back to the theatre. At 10.15, the doors opened and the audience flooded out onto the surrounding streets. Many joined the queue for the taxis that had been waiting outside the doors, while others headed for the tube. Yet more simply dispersed on foot into the surrounding streets, keen to enjoy a stroll late on a spring evening.

They followed the crowds to Piccadilly Circus, which was open this evening but, seeing no point in recreating an impossible journey, they walked back to Victoria and caught the train home. Saric spent most of the journey with his face buried in his phone. As they passed through a series of tunnels that evidently cut off his internet connection, he looked up at Rob. "It's possible you know."

Saric had a habit of assuming that Rob could read his mind. "What is?"

"The train from Paddington to Reading takes less than half an hour. He could have got from the theatre to Reading, killed Jane and been back in London to get the last train home. We'd need to check the trains ran on that day, of course. Sense Check can deal with that, but it's possible."

"But why? We've got nothing that indicates a motive, and even if we had that, does he really seem like the sort of man capable of planning this? Isn't it more likely that he just went home like he said he did?"

"Of course, it's more likely, but we can't just consider that. If it's possible that he did it then we should follow up. When we get home, I'll ask Sense Check to verify the potential journeys and then I think we should visit him again."

As they had had a drink in London, they chose to walk home from their nearest stations. The long day had turned to night and a light rain was gently falling. Saric did not mind the rain, which was badly needed. June had been unusually hot, and he could feel the tired, dusty air clearing around him as he walked. It amazed him how such a small amount of rain could make all the other passengers leaving the train turn to taxis, but he smiled as he thought about them standing in the queue while he walked along empty paths. His phone interrupted his contemplation.

"Saric, I know it's late, but I thought you would want to hear this tonight. I've had a look at the records on your murder victim." It was the lab tech, he sounded tired. Saric was pleased that he had not waited.

"No problem, I'm still up, thank you for calling so quickly. What did you find?"

"The drug in her system was Alfentanil. It's a strong painkiller that is only available on prescription, and even then, it's tightly controlled. This isn't the kind of thing they prescribe for a bit of back pain. The post-mortem found that the victim had been injected with a massive dose."

"Is that what killed her?"

"No, it probably would have, but it doesn't look like she was given enough to kill her straight away. She would have spasmed, but in the end it was suffocation."

"One more thing . . ." Saric started. There was a sigh at the other end of the phone, and he knew he was pushing this favour too far. He had agreed, after all, that the lab tech had settled his debt. "Is there a black market for this stuff?"

"There's a black market for all controlled substances, if you look hard enough."

As Saric ended the call, he wondered what this could mean and how it fit with the other facts they had established.

CHAPTER 34

Early the next morning, Rob and Saric were standing at Colin's front door. Saric had grown tired of listening to well-rehearsed speeches, so they planned to catch him before work in the hope that he may be forced into some honesty. Rob thought that this plan was unlikely to succeed; men like Colin planned scenarios in so much detail that they were unlikely to be caught by surprise, but he also couldn't see Colin as a suspect, so he thought there was nothing to be lost through trying.

Rob pressed the bell, which chimed loudly, and the men waited for several minutes before Colin answered.

"Gentlemen! What an unexpected surprise!"

Colin's smile was broad, but it did not spread as far as his eyes. He kept his hand on the door, blocking their entry. It was friendly, but the meaning was clear; Colin was not at all happy to see them.

"Good morning, Mr Edwards." Rob returned the smile. "We are very sorry to bother you this early, but we were hoping to pick your brains on a couple of matters relating to Jane Evans. We wanted your opinion on a few things and, as your observations so far have been incredibly helpful, we hoped to trouble you just a little further."

This confused Colin. He was ready for confrontation with Saric but flattery from Rob was too tempting. After hesitating slightly, he opened the door.

"Of course, come in. Anything I can do to help the justice process. Do excuse the mess, I was just having breakfast."

They walked through a short hallway past a couple of closed doors into a living room that also held a dining table. The mess, as far as Rob could see, constituted of a single plate with some half-eaten toast and a cup of tea.

He should see my place, he thought.

The bungalow was not large, but it was well maintained, although the furnishings were rather old fashioned, more the sort of thing you would expect to see at your grandmother's than at a single man's place.

They accepted tea and the three men sat around a large round coffee table. Rob wanted Colin to feel comfortable and able to confide in them.

"We have some questions about your impressions of Spencer and Evans, you know, the way they run the business," Saric started. Rob smiled inwardly. Saric could not care less about anyone's impressions and much less Colin's.

"But before we get to that, I thought I'd mention that we saw the play you recommended," Rob lied. "It really is excellent, isn't it? How did you hear about it?"

"I like to keep my finger on the pulse of the major theatres. I've moved to Sussex temporarily, but I'll be back in London soon, so I need to keep my knowledge up to date."

"And what do you do for work?"

"I've taken a job as a Financial Controller of a manufacturer in the industrial estate. It's not really the right fit for me, I'm a bit over-qualified to be honest, but it was available when I got to Sussex and it lets me pursue my other interests in the theatre."

"What brought you to Sussex?" Rob asked casually.

"My mother. She's unwell and can't cope on her own anymore, so I've moved in to look after her. This is her house. I was renting a place in

London and when I return, I expect to be able to buy somewhere, so leaving my place there wasn't too difficult and worth it if it keeps my inheritance. My mother keeps threatening to leave it all to some terrible charity that rescues cats."

"Is your mother here?"

"Yes, but she stays in bed. She's taking quite a lot of strong medication and she rarely makes it out of her room these days. That's her room, down the corridor." He nodded back towards the front door.

"And in London, what did you do there?"

"I ran the finance team in one of the big theatres. It was a much better job, really, but the commute wouldn't work from here. I stay in touch, though, and I'm sure they will give me the job back when I get back to London."

"When we were at the theatre, we bumped into your friend Jenny. She sends her regards. She was worried about you, actually. She said she was expecting to meet you after the show, but you didn't turn up."

Colin's whole body tightened, almost imperceptibly, but strongly. His face did not move. "Yes, it's a bit awkward really. I think she was hoping for rather more than a catch up between colleagues, if you see my meaning. I'm not proud of it, but I just left rather than let her down. She's a bit like that and well, with Sarah . . ."

He did not finish his sentence.

Saric stood up. "Shall I get us some more tea?" he said.

Rob had barely touched his cup but knew better than to point this out and jumped in to say "yes" before Colin could intervene. Saric left the room to the kitchen next door, and Rob pressed on with their questions.

"I know Saric has more questions about Jane, but I think we should wait for him for those. We went to the pub three doors down from the theatre before the performance. It was lovely. Have you been there?"

"No, I don't think so. I just went straight to the theatre when I went there. I spent an hour in the bar. I thought it might be nice to see some of my old colleagues."

Saric returned with more tea and they continued to ask Colin some questions about Jane and Tony. The way Colin explained it, he was their most important client, having taken them the work from the theatre and the firm he was working for. They knew from the firm's records that this was not true but now did not seem like the time to raise this.

Colin thought Jane was a good accountant, but he seemed far more impressed by Tony, although he hadn't had much first-hand experience of working with him. Saric thought this was likely to have far more to do with the adviser's gender than with their capabilities. Tony looked like what people like Colin thought accountants should look like; middle-aged men with grey hair and a large waistline could be trusted far more easily than women.

They gave Colin a few more minutes to show off before Rob said, "Colin, thank you, I'm sure you're very busy, so we won't hold you up any longer, but your contribution has been invaluable."

Colin beamed, looking very pleased with himself. "Any time, gentlemen, and if you would like anymore insider tips on the arts then just let me know."

The door had barely closed on the bungalow before Saric whispered to Rob, "We need to speak to Grace urgently."

CHAPTER 35

"What did you find?" said Rob.

"You remember I thought that Deputy Chief Stephens had kept something back from us? The liquid they found in the room, which wasn't blood or vomit and was on the pillow used to suffocate Jane Evans, was clearly something the police thought important. It got me thinking when Phillip told us they were asking about the drug history of his girlfriend. If Jane was murdered and there was some foreign substance on the pillow, drugs are likely.

"Jane Evans is no drug addict, so that takes us to only one conclusion. Someone else put the drugs into her, at a level that would send her straight into convulsions. But you don't go to the trouble of injecting someone with a lethal dose of opiates, only to then suffocate them with a pillow. The injection did not go as planned. You see, this was not a seasoned assassin. A true killer would know what the drugs they were using would actually do or go straight to the suffocation. It would never be both; it's a waste of effort. This was an amateur; and someone who wanted to inject their target whilst they slept, sit back and watch them die, and then slip out into the night.

"But the thing that doesn't make sense is the type of drug that was used. I called in a favour at the lab and it wasn't some easily available street drug. This was a prescription painkiller. You can access it if you look hard enough. Maybe Phillip would have gone to the trouble of asking his girlfriend to provide this specific drug, but why bother when any number of other substances would be more easily available and do the same job? Much more likely the killer had this drug to hand."

"That feels like a lot of leaps of faith for you, Saric," said Rob.

"Granted, but I've been doing this for a long time, and I set a lower bar of suspicion for a liar. And Colin is full of shit. And do you want to know what I found in his kitchen? Alfentanil, a prescription painkiller opiate. The same drug that the police found in Jane."

"OK," said Rob, raising an eyebrow. "But there's one thing still missing, isn't there? Motive."

"Yes," said Saric.

"And you think Grace can give it to you?"

"Maybe."

"OK," said Rob again. And as an afterthought, "Do you really think this tubby little man could go through with killing someone? I find him sort of endearing."

Saric put his hand on Rob's shoulder. "My friend, everybody you have ever met is capable of murder. You just need to give them a good enough reason."

Rob thought on that for a moment. Before his life was destroyed, he would have said he could not take a life. Now he knew he could do it without hesitation. If it meant resolution. Saric saw his friend's mind drift, and he knew where it was going. Like so many times before, he pulled Rob back to the now.

"Will you phone Grace, please?" Saric said, explaining what he wanted to know.

Rob smiled. "Does she still owe us anything, or are we asking for a favour?"

"Half a day," said Saric.

Rob put in the call. Grace's PA still had instructions to put their calls straight through, although Grace explained to Rob that this would be the last time. Unless Saric called her himself, of course.

"Grace, we've been following up on this chap, Colin, who was occupying Jane's time. We don't believe what he told us about why he was doing this. Is there anything in the documents you took that could uncover what they were really talking about? You know we've already run checks on the digital data."

"Well, there's a stack of handwritten notebooks. They won't be in any of the digital info. I'll get one of the boys in the office to have a look in there. Anything specific to focus them on?"

"No, just the dates. I just need to know why Colin was really bothering her that week."

"Fine. Will he ever phone me?" said Grace.

"I'm not sure. Do you want him to?"

"Do bears shit in the woods? Of course, I want him to. Listen, Rob, do me a favour, get that friend of yours to take a bit of time out. Let him figure out what matters. And get him to bloody well call me!"

"OK," said Rob, smiling. *Poor Saric*, he thought, *she would eat him alive.*

First thing the following morning, one of Grace's team emailed Saric. The notebooks had been easy to follow, with dates at the top of each page, client names underlined and notes made mostly in long hand. Grace's colleague had attached photos of the pages he thought relevant.

A couple of weeks before Colin demanded an after-hours meeting, Jane had written:

<u>South Downs</u>

Gift Aid reclaim – reconcile – need file note for one-off jump. Call Treasurer.

Three days before the Colin meeting, she seemed to have made a note of a call:

<u>Colin S. Downs</u>

One-off. Old contacts came good??? "Not authorised" to speak to the tax authorities.

The day they met:

South Downs – Treasurer (Colin Edwards)

Still no claim form. Get from elsewhere – admin? Review in full at year end? Check reporting requirements. Fraud?

Interesting, thought Saric. Looks like Colin was up to something after all. *I need to know what Gift Aid is*, he thought. But first, he had an appointment at Rob's house.

When he arrived, Saric let himself in. Rob was in the lounge watching the opening discussions of daytime TV. He had been working out. Saric looked over at the screen and felt a sense of sorrow for every lost soul that wasted a single moment of their one shot at life sucked into this drivel.

Saric was there to help Rob set up a state-of-the-art home detection system. Not quite the bespoke, fully integrated, intelligent house Saric had built for himself, but enough to provide Rob some comfort that he would get woken up before finding some goon standing over his bed in the middle of the night.

Rob welcomed Saric in.

"Thank God you're here," he said. "I was about to find out which tone of lipstick will lift my complexion."

Over the next few hours, Rob and Saric went around most of the house adding detectors to all the ground floor entrances, with Saric making notes of other home security improvement options.

"The windows at the front of the house should be upgraded; they're too easy to force. These ones are fine. Why did you only upgrade the back of the house?"

"We did it when we extended the upstairs. I told you about that before, remember? We would have done the front at the same time, but the inheritance didn't stretch to it. If we hadn't got that, we wouldn't have been able to do anything, not on the money we were making then."

"Oh, yes," said Saric. Saric stood in thought for a moment. "I wonder what Colin has planned for his inheritance," he said.

"Yeah," said Rob, "if the cats don't get it! Poor Colin, that would really screw over the little man."

Saric explained what he had learned from Grace's colleague earlier. I don't know what it means, but if it's fraud, that's money. Why would

Colin want money if his mother's about to leave him a stash?"

"Maybe she really has left a wedge of it to the cats and he's still working on her," said Rob.

"How would we know?" said Saric.

"We'd have to see the will. That would give you a list of all the people she wants her money to go to."

"Yes, I suppose it would," said Saric. "It's basically your final list of the most important people in your life, isn't it?"

"I guess."

"Let's get on with this," said Saric, returning to the task in hand.

Saric had brought some motion sensors with him, and he gave Rob the job of installing them downstairs while he worked his way round alarming the upstairs windows. If anyone did force them open, Rob would get plenty of warning.

More importantly, something in what Rob had said had triggered an idea, one that concerned his friend, but which required more thought before he could discuss it with him. He thought there might be some documents of use in the spare room, but he wanted to find them without alerting Rob.

Taking care to ensure that Rob was occupied with the sensors, Saric made his way to the first floor. Four doors led off a small landing. One of these was to a room he had only entered once, when he had first visited for Rob's case. Since then, there hadn't been a need to, and pretending the room was not there had worked for them both.

Saric was most interested in the contents of the spare room, so he started his work in there. He had helped Rob dump boxes of paperwork here after the first phase of his case. He guessed they had not moved since.

On entering the room, he was surprised to see that the bed had recently been slept in; a half-full glass of water and a novel were sitting on the bedside table. He had assumed that Rob would be using the bedroom, and it was another sign of the depth of his friend's grief, and that five years had not been long enough to heal sufficiently that he could bear to do that. Sadness mixed with frustration at his own failure, but he pushed this aside; there was work to be done.

After spreading a few items out to give the impression that he was working on the installation, he stepped over to the side of the room, where a number of boxes of paperwork had been pushed onto the shelves of a tall bookcase. He recognised much of it.

Wills. A list of the most important people in your life. As far as he was aware, Saric had never been the beneficiary of a will. He had not had that kind of life. Wills were for people with families, and possessions. But Helen had been the beneficiary of a will. Enough to pay for an extension. That was the sort of money that meant she was important to the person who gave it to her; it was not just a token but a significant sum.

Helen had been brought up by her maternal grandmother, after her mother had died when she was a teenager. Her father had never been in the picture and, as far as anyone knew, was not even aware that Helen existed. When Helen's grandmother had passed away a few years before Helen disappeared, she had left her enough money to pay for the extensive home improvements. Rob had told Saric all this when they first met, when he was describing the members of their family.

Speaking to Colin earlier had made Saric think. He had never actually seen the will, and that was a loose end.

He worked methodically through the boxes. The ones he had seen before were neatly organised. There was very little order in the others, and it took a while. As he worked, he picked up various documents, some of which he had seen before and others that were new to him. Near the bottom of one box, he found a large open envelope franked with the name of a small law firm. The envelope contained a bundle of papers and, in neat writing, which did not belong to Rob, was printed ALICE'S ESTATE. Not wanting to risk Rob seeing what he was doing, he tucked the envelope and the other papers he had found to be of interest into his bag and pressed on with fitting the window alarms. He was tempted to make an excuse to leave Rob to finish the security arrangements and head straight home, but his friend's safety needed to be prioritised over a long shot on a case, no matter how important.

After finishing the spare room, he took a deep breath before entering the master bedroom. The room was only slightly larger than the spare room, but it had been decorated with care and kept tidy. Unlike the spare room, it was clear that this bed had not been slept in for some time. Some items of Helen's jewellery and makeup sat on a small dressing table, along with an almost empty bottle of perfume. Next to it was a picture of the three of them when their son was born. Not wanting to disturb anything, as if even his presence in the room might disrupt the still air that was held in suspension in the silence, Saric worked quickly to install the alarms.

Finally, he opened the door to Rob's son's room. Saric was not sentimental, but even for him this was hard. The boy would be eight now, but in this room, he was still three. Saric knew that Rob would sometimes find the courage to sit in here, when he could face the pain. Or perhaps because of the pain, like some kind of punishment. The room was tidier than it had been when Saric had first visited in the aftermath of the disappearance. The chaos of soft animals and toy cars left by a three-year-old had been replaced by order, but the same toys now lined the shelves.

Once the first floor was secure, Rob returned to his friend, who was sitting silently in the armchair. Of course, he knew where Saric had been, and Saric could see that even the thought of him entering that room caused Rob pain. Sometimes, Saric could deflect this, change the subject, discuss a case, but now the only thing he could find to do was sit in silence beside Rob and support his grief for his missing wife and child.

After some time, Rob spoke, his voice flat. "Grace called."

"Oh." Saric wanted to know what Grace had said, but he did not want to push Rob to converse until he was ready. Even though this was murder, solving the case was not as important as looking after his friend.

"She says this Gift Aid thing is big. Something about crimes, and prison sentences."

"Oh."

"She says she will explain it to you, but that you are not owed any more time, and if you want to know you will have to buy her dinner."

CHAPTER 36

Saric needed Grace, and he knew it. He definitely needed her to fill him in on this accounting stuff. If that was all, why had he dug out his best shirt and cleaned his shoes? He was not sure.

He got to the restaurant exactly on time and immediately felt uncomfortable, as Grace was yet to arrive. He had to make a decision between waiting at the bar or going to the table. Neither option seemed satisfactory. Waiting at the bar, he thought, made him look a bit pathetic. He looked at the other people lined up there. There were people waiting for their dates to arrive, all glued to their phones in an attempt to look like they weren't alone. There were two couples, both loading up before dinner.

What the hell is wrong with these people? thought Saric.

The alternative, waiting at the table, meant constantly looking up at every person entering the restaurant, only to look away again when it was not her, like some sad loser preparing to be stood up. And explaining to the waiting staff that he was a little early, even though he was not, and they could not care less.

He considered walking out and coming back, but that would be the weirdest of all the options, so he settled for taking a seat at the table. He ordered a glass of water, explaining, unnecessarily, that he would have a proper drink when his guest arrived.

He could have taken out his phone, and although it would have been helpful to look up several things right now, he did not want to look like one of those sorts of people when Grace walked in. So, he just sat and thought.

After he had left Rob's house, he had gone straight home with the paperwork that he had gathered up and immediately opened Helen's grandmother's will. It was a data point that had never come up before, so it had never got into Sense Check. Rob had clearly never opened it. Why would he? It was years ago and how could it be linked to his wife's disappearance? Maybe in those early days Saric would have ignored it too. But now, after five years of working and reworking the data, exhausting the dead ends, churning the police information and trying every possible way he could think of to get some sort of angle on this, it felt like a big stone unturned.

As he opened the will, he felt his heart race. 'Please, please give me something,' he said out loud. 'Anything. I have to close this case. There has to be a resolution. He deserves this. Of all the cases, this cannot be the one that is beyond me.'

And there it was. For the first time in the five years that this case had consumed him, Saric had a new name. Helen's grandmother, Alice, had left £25,000 to a woman called Julia Hawkins, "Should she return to the UK to collect it in person."

He put the woman's name straight into Sense Check but got nothing useful back, though he discovered the legal firm that handled the will was still operating. He got a list of current and retired partners, with details of profits, and so on. He would see them in person as soon as possible. Rationally, he knew this remained a long shot, but it was something, and he would take everything from it that he could.

Grace walked in. Saric was a little taken aback. She looked different to normal, but not in a bad way. No, definitely in a good way. He realised suddenly that he had never seen her outside of work before. She was always well dressed in their meetings but in a formal, tailored way. As she walked towards the table, he recognised that the raw power of her work persona was a little diluted by a femininity that until now he had only vaguely been aware of. She wore a knee length dress made from a material that seemed to float around her as she walked, and her usual tailored suit jacket had been replaced by one in deep blue denim. Her dark hair was messy but somehow deliberately so, as if she had styled it that way. Saric had no idea how she would have achieved this, but he enjoyed the effect. *Wow*, he thought, *she's absolutely stunning.*

He stood up and then realised he wasn't sure why. Should he shake her hand, kiss her on one cheek or both, or do nothing? Oh crap. Grace dealt with it. She put one hand on his shoulder and kissed him lightly on the left cheek. She smelled perfect.

"Hello," he said. He felt like he was supposed to say something else next, but his mind was blank, so he just sat down.

"It's lovely to see you out, Saric," she said.

"Thank you." That did not seem quite right, either.

"Even if I had to bribe you to get you here," she added.

She had a glint in her eye, which let him know she was gently toying with him.

"You look very–" Saric stalled.

Why on earth did I start that sentence? he thought.

"–nice."

"Thank you," she said with a warm smile.

"Let me tell you what you want to know, and then you're going to talk with me about other things for the rest of the meal. But don't worry, Saric, I'll try and be worthy of your attention."

Saric felt himself going a little red. *Why would this woman be interested in me?* he wondered. Maybe it would be fun to find out. But Grace was right, it would be good to get the matter in hand out of the way.

"Gift Aid," said Grace, "is a tax refund system. If you give money to charity, the charity can reclaim some money from the government. There are certain rules, of course; you have to be a UK taxpayer, and you have to fill in your details on a form. The charity keeps a record of who you are, and how much you gave, and passes that onto HM Revenue, then they pay the charity the money. It has been abused, though. It seems it's been a good place for people to rip off the system. The

304

Revenue pay out the claim before they have done anything more than a basic check. They often do a more thorough check later, and they seem to have a pretty good track record of catching up with people in the end. Every year, the Revenue publish their top cases of tax avoiders they have sent to prison, and there's nearly always a Gift Aid fraudster in the mix. It's good PR to catch these people; they have stolen from both the government and charity. If your man Colin was involved in defrauding the Gift Aid system, he would be taking a big risk."

"How do I check?"

"I'm not sure really, but if I were you, I would start by getting hold of the Gift Aid claim form that raised Jane Evans's suspicions. That should include the names of the donors. You might be able to check into those people and see if they are genuine."

"OK, thanks."

Saric thought he had taken it all in, but his mind was starting to wander a little. Despite her high-powered role, Grace had laughter lines that gave a hint of another side to her. He wondered if he could make her laugh. Her eyes were drawing him in. She really was beautiful.

They ordered their food. Grace let Saric choose the wine, and she was happy with his choice. They discussed wine, art, European politics, why things are the way they are and how it would be better if they weren't. Grace never asked Saric about himself, and he felt grateful for that. She displayed no interest in understanding him, looking after him, or showing him off.

I could definitely do this again, he decided.

CHAPTER 37

By the time Rob arrived at work the next morning, Saric was already at his desk. He had spent a couple of hours trawling the internet for any clues as to who Julia Hawkins might be. The phrase in the will that struck him as odd was, "should she ever return to the UK". It was possible that Alice and Julia had simply lost touch and that the gift was contingent on being able to find her, but something in the way the condition had been expressed made Saric think that maybe Alice knew where Julia was. Why else would she think she was overseas? But if Alice knew where Julia was, then why could the gift not be transferred to wherever that was, as part of distributing the assets? The thought process was circular and Saric was no further on when Rob placed the large mug of coffee on his desk.

"How was dinner?" Rob was barely hiding a smile.

"Very nice, thank you. The Gift Aid angle is worth looking into."

This was not what Rob was asking about but avoiding answering the question seemed like the easiest approach for Saric.

"I wasn't asking about Gift Aid. How was Grace?"

Of course, Rob was not going to let him get away with it that easily.

Before he could stop himself, a smile spread across Saric's face, as he remembered the night before. "She was great, we had a really good evening."

"Is that all you have to say?"

"Yes, that's all." But he was still smiling. Rob gave him a sceptical look and Saric knew they would be revisiting this subject later. He hoped by then he might have thought of something more coherent to say.

"We do need to look at this Gift Aid thing, though. If there really was a fraud, like Jane seemed to be thinking, it would have been really serious. If Colin was involved, it could have meant prison for him. If that's the case, it might be enough to convince the police of a motive."

"So, what do we need?"

"Some evidence. So far, it all makes sense, but there is nothing to prove Colin has done anything wrong, and so there's no evidence of a motive. Grace said there should be a form somewhere that the charity would have submitted to the tax man that lists all the people who donated. If we can find that, maybe we can look into the donors and find something on one of them."

"Right, that makes sense, but where would we find that form?"

"Colin's the treasurer, so I suppose he would be in charge of submitting returns to the tax man, so either at his home or maybe at his office. I don't think Colin's going to let us in there again, though, so I was thinking that maybe we could access the property while he's out. Otherwise, perhaps we could contact the Revenue, pretend to be Colin and ask for a copy of the return. I don't know, maybe we could say we've lost it."

"Saric, don't you think you might be complicating things a bit?"

"What do you mean?"

"Well, they're all great ideas, and maybe they would work, but to be honest, they sound dangerous and I'd say almost certainly illegal."

Saric still looked blank.

"So, I'm not saying we don't do that, but maybe we should see if we can find an easier way that's less likely to get us arrested."

"Yes, but I don't see how else we can get the document; we need access to the office."

"Perhaps," said Rob, "but aren't most things done online these days? And if Jane was looking at the matter, isn't it possible she had a copy? And don't you have a download of all her files and emails sitting right in front of you?"

Saric looked at his screen as he caught up with Rob's thinking. He did not respond but started typing a search for any file containing the keywords "theatre" and "Gift Aid". He wasn't sure why he had missed that. He was usually so efficient and focused. But there was Helen and there was Grace, and something in him wanted to act instead of sitting behind a desk.

There was nothing in any of the file names, but a few emails included the right words. Saric flicked through them until he found one that looked promising. It was a long trail, where Jane had requested an extensive list of documents from Colin so that she could examine the accounts. Colin had said he would get his administrator to forward on the documents, and a couple of days later an email with a number of attachments had been sent to Jane.

Hi Jane,

Please find attached the documents you have requested for your review of our accounts. I've attached the following:

- *Draft accounts*

- *VAT returns*

- *Gift Aid claims submitted during the year.*

If you need anything else, please let me know.

Kind regards, Sarah Fletcher

Saric opened the attachment called 'Gift Aid claims'. It was a large spreadsheet with a long list of names, dates and amounts. This looked promising. There were sixty-five lines, most for donations of less than £100. The exception was a few weeks where the charity had received much larger donations.

First name	Last name	House Number/Name	Postcode	Donation date	Amount (£)
William	Collins	8	BN4 9NA	02/01/19	25,000
George	Shaw	The Spinney	PO4 9AX	04/04/19	17,850
Henry	James	87A	RH3 0PA	29/04/19	50,000
George	Arliss	4	RH13 8ND	10/10/2019	12,000

It seemed odd that all these donations had been received in such a short space of time. Of course, it could be a coincidence. Saric thought the arts must be the sort of area where wealthy people would donate to impress their friends, but the timing was strange.

As Rob went to collect the post that had just been delivered, Saric tasked Sense Check with looking at the donors to see if it could connect any of them to other fraud. It was a long shot but worth a try. If it did not work then they could try confronting Colin with it anyway, hoping he would be scared or confused enough to come clean, but it would be a bluff and he thought it unlikely that Colin would be fooled without some detail to convince him.

Saric's letterbox was on the wall next to his front door. The post fell into a reinforced box. Rob put in the four-digit code and took out the day's delivery. When he first saw this set up, he thought it was borderline paranoid, but he had gotten used to it since. Now that someone had broken into his house, he had a renewed appreciation for Saric's logic; if you can take away a risk, do so.

In these days of electronic communication, almost all the post both he and Saric received was junk. This pile was no different; charities Saric had once given money to asking for more, a local newsletter with a front page still complaining about local planning requests. All junk except for one polythene envelope with a handwritten address. He scooped them up, shut the box and went back to Saric in his office.

He threw the letters onto a sideboard, announcing them as irrelevant.

"This might be more interesting, though," he said, and dropped the package onto Saric's desk.

Saric was distracted by the computer screen, but he picked up the package and tore the top off, allowing the contents to fall out.

Rob took a step back and stopped breathing for a moment. It was Squashy Dog. Someone – someone Rob instantly knew must die – had pulled the head off his son's beloved stuffed toy. The body and head lay on the desk next to a handwritten note. Rob felt like someone had reached straight into his heart and was crushing it – and laughing at him as they did so. His mind shot in several directions at once, with none of the thoughts forming fully before the next one pushed it aside . . . Dad. That torn apart remnant on Saric's desk was a container for his dad's love for his grandson.

Rob thought, *I'll find who did this and give him to Dad. Then they will know what this means. We'll tear him apart together. What about when my son comes home? Squashy Dog is going to help him know he is home. Safe. Not now. Even fixed, it would be ruined . . . Kill the bastard. Rip him apart. It was the one thing. Helen will know I couldn't keep the one thing safe. I couldn't keep them safe. I've failed them again. Someone is going to pay.*

Saric looked at his friend. He was not going to snap him out of this one with a change of subject. He would have to deal with it head on. Rob was pacing now.

"Sit down, Rob," said Saric.

Rob sat down out of instinct.

"Look at me!"

Rob did not take his eyes off the toy. He looked like he wanted to pick it up but could not bring himself to reach out for it. Saric picked up the note.

Rob was breathing fast. He looked at the note in Saric's hand. Saric looked at him.

Only the truth will do here, he thought.

Saric read it out. "'Next time it will be the boy', it says."

Rob laughed out loud. "Good luck with that! Ha!" he sounded hysterical.

"I did not think it would come to this, Rob," said Saric. "I'm sorry."

Rob looked Saric straight in the eye. "You don't need to be sorry. But they will be."

Saric thought for a moment. Rob had come a long way in the five years since they had met. He had learnt how to navigate some of the more undesirable elements of the criminal world. And he had become impressive physically. He was a handful in a fight. Maybe he could take Jim Callagher out, but he would never do it and walk away untouched, not without Saric's help.

"It's a cuddly toy, Rob," he said. He did not want to say it. He knew it carried a lot of emotional attachment. "We have to keep this in context."

"What bloody context, Saric? My boy's gone. My wife's gone. No one knows where. Or why. It's been five years." Tears formed in his eyes. "I keep pretending we're going to find them, but I don't know if even I believe it anymore. I will not let the memory of them go undefended. I couldn't stop them from leaving, or help them, or understand, but I can at least live with a memory I can be proud of. This snivelling little bastard will not take that from me. It's all I have left!"

Full tears were rolling down his cheeks now, although he had not noticed.

"No," said Saric. "If it was time to give up on your wife and son I would say so. But it's not. I have not given up. We do not have enough data to give up." He took a piece of paper out of his drawer and pushed it across the desk at Rob.

"Look at it," he said.

Rob seemed to have forgotten how to read altogether. "What is it?"

"It's your wife's grandmother's will. We never looked at it at the time. Why would we? Every other line we took supported Helen being alone before you met, apart from her grandmother. No family except Granny Alice, and she's long gone. Always dead ends. Sense Check did not challenge it. But there is someone else, Rob. Have you ever heard of Julia Hawkins?"

Rob's mind was jolted out of his despair. He seemed to refocus, and he wiped the tears from his eyes. Saric made a point of not noticing them.

"No, never heard of her. Why?"

"She is in Helen's grandmother's will. And it's odd, because this Julia only gets the money if she returns to the UK. Do you see, Rob, this is new data? We need to find this person. We are not ready to give this up. And I am going to need you focused on what matters. This toy," he put his hand gently on the mutilated stuffed dog, "can be replaced. You think

317

your dad wouldn't tear this into a thousand pieces to hold his grandson in his arms again? Don't you dare give up on this now."

Saric leaned forward in his chair, reached over the desk and put his big hand on Rob's forearm.

"Let's see if we can get your family back," he said, "and then we'll figure out how to bring a reckoning to Jim Callagher. Please."

"OK," Rob said.

Saric sat back again. Rob looked drained. Saric made them coffee.

CHAPTER 38

The next few hours were tense. They sat in Saric's office while he worked hard on the computer and Rob sat impatiently, silently tearing the corners of the notebook in front of him. Saric let him be there. There was no use asking him to work, but he could not let him go off on his own. Not where he could not keep an eye on him.

Rob was an anomaly to Saric. It was not that Saric disliked people. In fact, on the whole he found them to be interesting, but he had never really had a friend before. Growing up, it had just been him and his father. He remembered having a vague awareness that other boys his age played football and went to parties, but that had just never been part of his life. They had spent weekends and holidays camping in the woods and hiking up mountains. It was always just the two of them. Looking back now, he could see this was unusual, but then it had been normal. He had never been lonely, and he hoped the same could be said for his father.

Then his father had passed away and he had fallen into the military. He was used to order and routine and his work gave him that. He had been good at it, very good, and he had been on operations with people whom he had quite literally trusted with his life. They had been a sort of family, perhaps, but not friends. He had not seen them since he had left the military.

After that, he had started investigating. There were lots of acquaintances and expansive networks of contacts. Favours were owed and favours were repaid. He had been successful, but he had done it alone.

And then one day, five years ago, Rob had walked into his office. Another client with a missing spouse and child. He had worked the case hard, following up on every lead he could find. Sense Check had been less advanced then, but they had crunched the data and found nothing. The numbers said that it was most likely Rob's wife had simply left him, taking their toddler son with her. It happened. Despite what crime novels might portray, most disappearances like hers were explained because the wife was unhappy and could not face telling her husband that it was over. Sometimes the husband deserved that treatment, often he did not, but it still happened.

The data told Saric to give up, and the numbers never lie. Except when they do. Something about Rob had made him reconsider. Something in the way he held onto the hope. Even when that made no sense at all. Even when the data told him that was the wrong thing to do. So Saric had persevered, never quite ready to say it was time to give up.

Rob had accrued so many hours owed that he practically became a fulltime employee; and having him there made Saric more successful. More cases were solved quicker, because Rob saw things he did not. He saw patterns in things that should not have patterns and emotions that could not be quantified on the facial recognition system. Saric knew that one day science would explain this, and that there would be an algorithm for what Rob could do, but for now that was too complex to program.

Over time, the work on Rob's case slowed, as Saric ran out of things to try. He didn't give up, but the hours Saric spent on the job were now fewer than the hours worked by Rob. Rob should have left then and gone back to his old life, but that life was not there anymore and Saric was better for having him around, so he started to employ him for real.

Over time, their relationship developed beyond work. They spent time together discussing other things. They disagreed a lot. Rob saw right and wrong as fixed, as if everything could be classified as one or the other, and this clouded his opinions. Saric saw those same concepts as variable, depending on circumstance, facts and outcome. But more often than not their conclusions were the same, even if the reasons were different.

And now, five years after Rob had first arrived at his office, Saric was sitting with his best friend, his only friend, and asking that man to trust him when he said that the right thing to do was to ignore the anger and leave Jim Callagher for later. And to ignore the pain and wait to follow the lead presented by the will, because right now, Sense Check had given them the evidence they needed to solve their latest case.

CHAPTER 39

SEPTEMBER 2017

Lunch was the least formal meal. All meals were collective, and since showing a gradual return towards a full acceptance of the truth, Martha had been joining the community. All tables seated thirteen: one Elder and twelve 'disciples' there to learn from them. Normally, an unmarried woman would not be allowed to sit on the same table as potential future husbands, but Martha's improvement seemed to be so closely linked to the efforts of Daniel that the Senior Elder had relaxed this rule, after he was told in prayer that a special case should be made on this occasion.

The children sat on a separate table, and Martha was kept at the other end of the room. The limited time she had with her son was excruciating, but also the worst possible step the community Elders could have taken in seeking to control her. Until she had her son back fully, she would resist everything. For her, this was the most unshakable truth there could ever be. She could only shoot the occasional glance at her son during mealtimes, or otherwise risk being taken back to her room. He did not usually look unhappy.

Is that what I looked like? she thought. Painful as it was, she was confident that she had some time to play with. With help and patience, she had been taught how to claim back a life for herself and find happiness. If this did not go on for too long, she felt sure she could do the same for her son. And if she could get him home, maybe she could still have her husband's help . . . if he could possibly forgive her. She shut down the thought of her husband. The guilt. She should have told him everything.

Elders would rotate tables to ensure that the community was able to receive the benefit of all their knowledge of the truth. Today, the Elder at the head of Martha and Daniel's table was a man she had known since she was a baby. As herself, she thought he was a total arsehole; pedantic, self-important and a bit too interested in the young men of the community. As Martha, she found him wise and venerable, and she tried hard to hang onto his every word.

"Today is Saint Basil's feast day," the Elder said, and he started to explain the important role Saint Basil had played in supporting the truth during the early days of the church.

Bloody hell, Martha thought, *Saint Basil. You've got to be joking.*

Basil! Seriously. Is there a single name that doesn't have a saint attached to it?

She found herself wondering if there was a Saint Kevin, or Lucas, or Sandra.

I bet there is, she thought.

Her concentration was wavering. The only Basil she had ever come across was the fictional Basil Fawlty from the TV show. It reminded her of laughing along to the sitcom with her adopted grandmother. It was a happy memory. She tried to pull herself back to the learnings they were receiving, but she had missed a large chunk of why she was supposed to care about the achievements of Saint Basil. The slightest loss of concentration could be a problem. As everyone else at the table was so engaged, one wandering mind stood out. She knew this very well, as she had been carefully drip feeding a reduction in the concentration lapses to support the cover story of a gradual 'recovery'. This one, though, was accidental, but it was too late to recover it.

"I wonder, Martha, if you perhaps know more than I about Saint Basil?" said the Elder. "Perhaps you have some great learnings of your own that you should share with us?"

What would Martha say? she thought.

"Of course not, my Elder, I know nothing of this great Saint Basil," Martha said, but she had not got the intonation quite right. It was so hard not to sound like she was mocking them.

"I dare say you do not. Your learnings have been so long interrupted," said the Elder.

"I am trying now," she said.

He looked unsure. "Perhaps," he said, "you could teach us many things from the time you were away?"

"I have learned only lies."

"Yes, you have. And worse, you have taught only lies. Your son knows nothing of the truth. Would you like to know what he told me today?"

Martha was unsure what the right answer was here, but she really did want to know. "Yes, I would," she said.

"He told me that his father knows there is no God, because his mother is the most perfect thing there could ever be."

The Elder let the comment hang there, whilst the rest of the table absorbed it.

"But do not worry, my child. I explained the truth."

"What truth?" said Martha. It just slipped out.

"The truth, my dear, that he has only one father, and that is the Great Lord. The man he thought was his father was not. It was a lie. If that wasn't the case, why isn't he here now? What sort of father does not take the trouble to look after his son? The Great Lord is his father now. I'm sure you would like to thank me for taking the time to support your child's education, Martha?"

She glanced towards the children's table. Her son was laughing with his new friends. And the realisation hit her. They were taking him. They might take her too, but he was what they really wanted. Her son. It was too much. She stood up, her shoulders held back, her piercing bright eyes fixed hard on the Elder. The meek subservience of Martha had entirely fallen away. She stood there, as the bold, determined, successful woman that she was.

"Now, Martha, listen—" started the Elder.

"No," she cut him off, "you listen to me, you pathetic sack of shit. This whole thing is bollocks. Over there is my son, not yours, not this community's. And he has a real father in the real world. And he's a thousand times the man you will ever be. And my name is not Martha. My name is Helen!"

CHAPTER 40

The light of the day was starting to accept that its moment had passed, and that the night must come. From Saric's office, he could watch the pinks and reds – and the colours he did not have the words for – mingle as the sun put itself to bed behind the hills of the South Downs. As he lost himself for a moment in the natural beauty, Sense Check alerted him to an output. It was not the answer Saric was expecting. He had put the odds of the program finding something unusual in the data at about sixty per cent. More likely than not, but far from certain.

If he had speculated, he might have expected some of the names on that list to be connections of Colin's, maybe a few names that would correlate with people with dubious tax histories. But Saric did not speculate so he would not admit to having thought those things. Sense Check's output was nothing like he had expected. In fact, Sense Check could find no record of anyone with any of those names living at the addresses provided.

This was not impossible. Sense Check's databases were not complete, being taken mostly from publicly available sources. It was possible that none of these people had any record anywhere in those systems. Possible, but statistically unlikely. Sense Check's own confidence calculations put the chances of it finding no reference at all to any of five randomly chosen UK individuals, based on names and addresses, at two point three per cent.

What was more interesting to Saric was what the names had in common. As part of its checks, Sense Check ran them through a number of internet search engines. One of them had returned a positive result. But these people could not be the donors, the five individuals named on the Gift Aid claim were some of the most influential playwrights of the nineteenth century.

Saric wondered whether this could be a coincidence. Some of the names on the list were quite common. It was not impossible that people sharing their names had donated. But combining the fact that Sense Check had not found the existence of these people in 2019, and that the list of names was otherwise connected, it all seemed too much to be a coincidence. And it was not just a random list of names; it was playwrights. This was what they needed. It wasn't proof, but it was close to it. There was enough to interview Colin again.

"We've got him!"

For a moment, he forgot that Rob's mind was elsewhere, but the blank look facing him as he grinned triumphantly was enough to remind him. "Colin. I think we have enough."

Saric explained the results he had just reviewed, while Rob tried hard to concentrate on what he was hearing. It was like he was listening to him from far away. He could understand the words, but they seemed disconnected. He willed his brain to start processing them. He needed to be professional. If this would help catch a murderer then it was important, and even if it did not, he owed it to Saric to try.

Saric had finished talking and was waiting for his response. He wished he could remember what Saric had just said. "It makes sense," he agreed, "and Colin seems the type to think he would be the only one who would connect those names. But I still don't understand why. Look at the man. He's living in his mother's spare room and he looks like he hasn't bought a new shirt in at least five years. He hardly seems like he's just come into fifty grand, does he?"

"That's why I need you in the room when we speak to him. I can handle the data, but I need your help with the motive." Saric paused.

"Rob, I know the timing is terrible, but we are under pressure to solve this. I think an innocent man is about to be charged with his wife's murder, but even with the new results, the police won't look at this. They think they have their man and that this is all circumstantial. We need a confession."

"A confession, eh?" said Rob. "Well, it looks like we have him for fraud at least. If that's right, that means prison. That should unsettle him, and it gives us something to work with."

Rob thought for a moment. He tried to build the picture of Colin as a killer in his mind. It did not come easily.

"You know, we've come at this the long way round. If it is him, he's covered it well. Assuming you're going to keep this clean, we're going to need an angle, or he'll clam up. Even if we get him right on the hook for fraud."

Saric nodded. "It would save a lot of trouble to get it over and done with now, though," he said.

"We'll think of something," Rob replied. He was keen to see this resolved so he could follow up his own case.

They summoned Colin to Saric's office. He was still pleased with himself for how he had helped them earlier in the week, and he came gladly. When he arrived, Rob answered the door.

Rob felt a sense of readiness coming from Colin. Like an actor waiting in the wings ready to step onto the stage. *Is he enjoying this?* he thought. *If he is, he really has no idea who he is dealing with*.

Rob was pleased that they had managed to allow him to feel this way, and he reached out his hand. Rather than observing his guest's grip, as he would usually do, he pushed his own hand hard into Colin's and clamped it just a little too hard. He held it just a little too long, all the while presenting a big warm smile. Colin's response to the confusing body language was to shrink away a little. Rob put his other hand on Colin's shoulder and ushered him in.

"Come in," he said. He did not move fully out of the way, so that Colin had to squeeze past him into the hallway. Rob looked down at Colin as he went past. Colin did not meet Rob's eye.

As Colin walked up the stairs, he seemed to regain his composure, as if meeting Saric would be easier. Rob noticed this and smiled to himself. Saric was about to end this podgy little man's life as he knew it, and then forget about him by next week, and he did not have a clue.

"Thank you for coming so quickly. As you know, we are trying to resolve the facts surrounding the murder of Jane Evans, and we think you might be able to help clarify a few points."

"Of course, anything to help. As a matter of fact, I'm very glad to be able to lend you my expertise, but I do think you boys might soon need to accept this one is beyond you. No offence, but crimes like these are complicated and need real experts to decipher them."

Saric's jaw tightened. How could this man sit here and taunt him like that? He would not have minded if he was a worthy adversary, but the man was a pompous idiot.

"Of course, we appreciate your help. We think we are close to resolving this matter. As you know, I will be recording this conversation and my software program will be monitoring what we say. I will try to keep it brief, but there are certain details we would like to discuss." Saric did not give Colin a chance to respond but pressed on with his first question. "Can you tell me a little about the finances at your charity?"

If Colin was worried, he did not show it.

"Yes, of course. I'm the treasurer, which means that I'm responsible for raising funds and spending the money we make."

Saric smiled, as he thought back to how Grace had dealt with Tony Spencer's equally patronising explanation. This discussion called for more patience.

"We are a charity, so most of our income comes from memberships and donations, although we raise lots from ticket sales these days. That's really improved since I took over as treasurer."

Sense Check flagged this as a lie.

"That sounds like a lot of work for you alongside your day job," Rob interrupted. His voice was flat but Saric was glad he was there.

"Well, yes, of course, but I make it work. It's important to give back, you know. And I have a team that work for me."

"Oh, really, can you tell me about them?" Rob continued.

"Well, there are two of them. They're only volunteers and they don't have official positions, but there's a lad that helps out a bit with the bookkeeping. He's hoping to get into finance when he finishes his A

Levels, so it's all good experience for him and then–" there was a slight hesitation in Colin's well-practised delivery "–there's Sarah. You've met her of course."

"What does she do?"

Colin weighed up his response before speaking. "She's just an administrator."

"Does your charity claim Gift Aid on its donations?"

Saric wanted to keep the discussion moving.

"Yes, we do, not very much, though. There are some processes that we have to go through to do so; it's all very complicated and quite boring actually."

Sense Check told Saric that the Gift Aid income was a significant portion of the charity's income. He knew this already, but it was reassuring that the program was working correctly.

"Do you know all your donors, the ones you claim Gift Aid from?"

"Most of them, yes. Most of our donations are from members, but it's not a requirement that we know people."

"Do you know George Shaw, for example?"

Colin's face dropped. This was not what he had planned. He must know by now that they had found him out.

"No, I don't think I do." His voice was casual but Saric noted the caveat "I don't think", as if he might need to revisit this statement later.

"Oh, that's interesting. He made a large donation to your charity last year. In fact, he was responsible for five per cent of your yearly income. I would have thought you would remember him."

"Ah, yes, we were very fortunate to receive donations from a number of philanthropists last year. They were all incredibly impressed with our production of *Twelfth Night* and were inspired to donate."

"Five of them, I can see, but you didn't meet them?" Saric pressed the point.

"Well, no, I didn't. And anyway, tax records are confidential. How did you get access to that information?" Colin was angry now.

"The information came to us as part of our investigation. It's interesting, though, because we haven't been able to track down any of these generous people to verify their donations, and we have evidence that Jane Evans was looking into the matter. Apparently, claiming Gift Aid from people that don't exist is fraud. That would be very serious. It would mean prison for the person who did it. I wonder what someone would do to avoid being found out?"

"I'm sure they exist. We have signed forms."

"But you have no proof of who completed them, do you? How do we know that you didn't complete them yourself?"

From the corner of his eye, Saric could see Rob. He was paying attention now and there was something on his mind.

"Saric, stop!" Rob was sitting forward in his chair. "We are missing something here."

What was Rob doing? They had their man. They had evidence of the lies; it was him.

"What on earth are you talking about?" He hoped Rob knew what he was doing here.

"We're looking in the wrong place, it's been in front of us all this time."

Colin was staring at Rob too. He had no idea, either.

"We have the Gift Aid claim form, but it wasn't Colin who submitted it. And the names of the donors are playwrights, and not even ones that normal people have heard of. They were put together by a real artist, someone who knows theatre really well."

"Yes, I suppose that's true."

Saric trusted Rob enough to let this play out, but he needed to keep it in hand. Rob was an uncertain element at the moment. Saric trusted him, but he also knew what participating in this discussion was costing him.

"I think we should call Sarah in," said Rob. "We should give her a chance to tell her side of the story before we take her to the police."

"There's nothing Sarah can tell you that I can't," said Colin. "She just does the administration."

"One of you must know who these donors are, and you just told us it's not you," said Rob.

Sense Check flagged to Saric that Rob's statement was not correct; Colin had in fact only stated that he had not met the donors, not that he did not know them. This sort of logical stretching could be very helpful at times like this, Saric decided.

"You're quite right. Sorry, I was getting a little muddled there. Of course, I knew who the donors were."

"All of them?"

"Yes."

"So, you can explain how George Bernard Shaw made a donation to the South Downs Theatre company this year, despite dying in 1950?"

"What are you talking about?"

"See," said Rob, turning to Saric. "Colin here knows nothing about this. We have the wrong person. It's Sarah we need to bring in."

Rob turned back to Colin. "I'm sorry, Colin. You have been very helpful to us, but I'm afraid you have been duped. Your friend and colleague Sarah is a fraudster, and we shall soon prove beyond doubt that she is also a murderer. She has been using your theatre group to commit fraud, and poor Jane Evans found out about it. It looks like Mrs Evans was onto it, and she was probably about to ask for your help, before Sarah took matters into her own hands."

"Life in prison," said Saric, to no one in particular.

"This is ridiculous!" announced Colin. "You can't just go after Sarah. She would never do anything like this. And anyway, she wouldn't know how. OK, OK, you've found out about the Gift Aid claim, but it was not really fraud. I'm going to put it all back the way it should be."

"How do you plan to do that? We have the records, and I bet an accountant could prove you received the money. That's fraud, and covering it up would be a motive for murder. We know that Sarah was speaking to Jane about Gift Aid; we have the emails to prove it."

"No, it wasn't her. Look, I can explain. Yes, I filed the claim. I made up the names, but it was only temporary. When my mother finally dies, I will use my inheritance to back it all out again. If the stupid old cow had just got on with it this would never have happened; they gave her three months nine months ago."

"You expect us to believe that?"

"It's the truth! The theatre was bust. We would have had to pull the show. I had to do something."

"It's a theatre. Does it even matter if it's there or not?"

"It wasn't for me. If we pulled the show, then Sarah wouldn't have been able to perform. She had worked so hard, and she was so happy in that role. She trusted me to keep things going. The show must go on. It was just a loan. I was going to put it all back."

"Sarah filed the claim, not you," said Rob. "She must have known what you were up to."

"She didn't know anything, she just sent what I told her to. It was nothing to do with her. You must keep her out of this. Please."

Colin looked desperate now. His eyes were pleading with Rob to intervene.

"The police won't believe that. She broke the law. She'll go to prison too. They might even go after her for the murder."

"Murder? Look, please, I've admitted to fiddling the books a bit, but I didn't kill her."

"Jane was onto you, wasn't she? She was going to the authorities and you had to stop her. We know about the drugs, Colin. We saw them in your kitchen when we were at your house, and there's a prescription for them, isn't there? Your mother is sick, she wouldn't notice if some of her painkillers went missing. It was cowardly, and it didn't work, did it? You had to suffocate her anyway."

Colin was fidgety. "I was at the theatre when she was killed. You spoke to Jenny. She saw me. I have an alibi."

"No, Colin, you don't."

There was a point in every case when Saric knew he had found his man, and this was it. Colin was grasping now, reacting to the accusations blindly. He had lost control. It was only a matter of time.

"What you have is an alibi at the start of the show. But there was enough time for you to sneak out, get the train to Reading and murder Jane."

"You have no evidence. I was at the theatre."

"You're right," said Rob. "We don't have any evidence that puts you there, but I bet we could find it."

343

The coldness in Rob's voice scared Saric. It did not sound like his friend.

"Some evidence is easier to find when you know what you are looking for. I bet if we tell the police which trains you could have caught, they could find you on the CCTV. Are you sure you weren't caught on them?"

Colin didn't respond. His face, which was usually so red, was completely without colour.

"And then there's Sarah, of course," Rob continued, "she's a suspect too. The police will want to interview her. I imagine they will turn up at her house, and I wonder what her husband will make of that, especially when he finds out what was going on between the two of you. I think he'll probably be very angry indeed. Unless, of course, we could tell the police who killed Jane in such a way that they didn't need to interview Sarah. Perhaps then her name could be kept out of it."

Colin looked up. His eyes met Rob's and an understanding developed between them. This was why Saric needed Rob. Sense Check had found the evidence, but it was Rob who understood what a man would do to protect the woman he loved.

Colin dropped his head slightly. It was an almost imperceptible nod, an acceptance that he was backed into a corner. He had been outsmarted and there was no move left to him but to accept his fate.

He looked at Rob. His expression was asking for help. Or at least some understanding. "I'm a good man really," he said. "I've never put a foot wrong in my whole life; not so much as a speeding ticket."

He looked at the floor and let out a long breath. "I know you think it's silly; amateur, pointless even. I've seen that look in lots of people like you over the years. But you're wrong, so wrong. Whenever a person walks on stage and gives all of themselves over to the role, to bring to life the playwright's imagined world, there's a magic in it. You must have seen that in Sarah. She has never had anything. Did you know that? She's been to the same hotel in Lanzarote on holiday for six years in a row. Imagine that. And with him pawing all over her. I wanted to take her to Paris and Prague and Milan. I've never been to these places. Never had a reason to, but with her . . . with her there would have been a reason.

"Yes, at last, I thought maybe I had a reason." He looked up suddenly, at Rob and then at Saric. "I could have had it all, you know. She would have come with me. We were in love, for God's sake. I just needed that little nest egg, a bit of security, a healthy balance sheet! And then it would have happened. I just needed a return on my investment. All those years looking after the stupid old cow, and all she had to do was die on time. And then it all went wrong. The scheme we invested the theatre's money in went bad. They would have shut us down and she wouldn't have been able to . . . I wouldn't . . . I could not let that happen to her. I would not let her down. I had to see her perform that role.

"So, I filled in the form. It was simple really. A couple of false names and there you go. Cash in the bank. Mother had weeks left; that's what they said. As soon as my money came through, I was going to correct the form with my own donation. Job done. Everything would be back as it should be. Sarah gets to perform her role, and we get to be together. Do you know where I wanted to go with her first?" He looked from Saric to Rob, as if they might know. "The New Forest. She said she'd always wanted to see a wild pony, so I was going to take her to the New Forest. That probably sounds stupid to you two, but that was what she wanted."

Rob and Saric allowed a period of silence while Colin collected his thoughts. The silence overpowered him.

"She was too bloody diligent, you know. Jane Evans. If she only had the common sense to trust me, she would still be here. Thirty years I've been working in finance. I didn't need her to validate my accounts. She was perfectly competent, of course, but really, checking up on my accounts. She should have known it was a waste of time. She was supposed to know it was a waste of time. But she didn't. And that was that. I told her I would put it all back as soon as my inheritance came through, but she kept banging on about her obligations and duties. It was too much. I didn't really care about me. You do know that? But she was going to ruin Sarah's dreams. How was I going to rescue her from her terrible life if I was in prison?"

He trailed off again and looked at the floor.

"I thought it would be easy. She told me all about being away for a couple of days, so I would know not to expect her to be around to respond to queries. She even told me what hotel she was staying at. Same every year, she said. I took a trip to my old theatre, got my ticket punched, went to the toilet and, as soon as I knew the staff would have gone off for a break, slipped back out. The only problem was that Jenny could not help herself but invite me for a drink. I knew I wouldn't make it back in time, but I could hardly say no. Anyway, I'm sure it's not the first time she has been stood up after a show. She's always after one man or another, and she's not subtle about it. I got back on the tube out to Paddington and bought a ticket to Reading, using cash at a machine.

"A hotel full of accountants; I knew I would fit right in. And everyone's always drunk at these things. The staff either hate them or couldn't care less about them. They certainly don't bother asking any questions. I found out from one of them what room Jane Evans was in and told another I had lost my key. Then all I had to do was put on some gloves and wait. She was out for ages; I hadn't expected that. But eventually she turned up. She was drunk and looked tired. She didn't look happy. To me, she never looked happy." Colin sighed again. "I didn't know how long to wait. How long does a woman take to get ready for bed? How should I know! To be safe, I waited a whole hour. When I crept in, she was fast asleep. Her room smelled nice." He shook off the memory, and then carried on. "I went to the library, you know, to look it all up. I didn't want to leave an internet history of the effects of an Alfentanil overdose. It was supposed to be lethal, but I hadn't really thought through how long it would take. You should have seen her. I slammed it right into her; I reckon it went straight into her heart. I thought she would just slip away, but she didn't. She shot up, spun round. Her eyes . . . her eyes were wide open, but not seeing anything . . . oh my God . . . she . . . that look. I grabbed a pillow and put it over her face. I couldn't look at that face and, well, she stopped. She stopped. And that was that.

"That was that," he said again. "It wasn't supposed to go this way. If my stupid mother had just died the way she was supposed to. If Jane had just trusted me. If . . ." he trailed off.

Saric leaned forward in his chair. "Colin," he said, "I have no sympathy for you."

Rob showed Colin out, whilst Saric called Deputy Chief Stephens. He arranged to meet Phillip the next day, and then he made his excuses and left Rob in the office to tidy up the files.

CHAPTER 41

Jim was tired as he drove his car through the automatic gates and onto his driveway. His day had been spent dealing with problems that should not have come up. As a young man, he had imagined that once he was in charge of his own business, he would spend his days having long lunches and playing golf. He had worked hard to get where he was, learning his trade and building the businesses up to a point where he should be able to enjoy himself. The reality was that none of his team was as competent as he was or worked as hard as he did, and that meant that his days were spent dealing with problems.

It was late now, and he was looking forward to getting home to his wife. He was later than he should have been, but he knew that she would not mind. She had known what to expect when she married him; his work was not exactly nine to five, and she enjoyed the benefits of his success. As he pulled his car to a stop outside the door, he could see the lights on in the pool house, where she would be swimming lengths.

He did not bother turning on the lights as he walked down the hallway and into the kitchen, intending only to grab himself a scotch before heading over to the pool to watch her swim. He put ice into a glass and pushed the freezer door shut behind him. As he turned away, something caught his eye. A shadow in the darkness. Someone was sitting at his dining table.

He almost froze. He had invested in a state-of-the-art security system. No one should be here.

"Good evening, Jim."

There was something familiar in that voice, a hint of an accent that he recognised.

"Saric. How–" he ran out of words.

"You know, you can spend all the money in the world on security, but it's really worth nothing if your wife doesn't switch it on."

He silently cursed her; he had warned her so many times. His business brought him into contact with lots of less than upstanding characters. He had enemies and there were people who would rather he was not around anymore. He also knew that those people would hurt his wife to get to him; he knew this because if it got him what he wanted he would do the same to them without a second thought.

351

"What have you done to her?" If he had hurt her, Jim would kill him right now.

"Nothing. She's swimming. I think this is between us, and I'd rather avoid bringing family into it."

Jim considered this man for a moment. He was difficult to assess. He was obviously physically impressive, but it was hard to place him. Jim could not have guessed how old he was or where that accent was from, beyond a general impression that it must be somewhere in Eastern Europe. Jim was strong and extremely capable of handling himself in a fight. He had got to where he was by out manoeuvring older, more experienced players, but there was something in this man's eyes that terrified him. A cold calculating rationality. Jim did not want to have to face him.

"What do you want?"

"I asked you to leave Rob out of this and you ignored me."

There was no use denying it; he had not exactly been subtle with his messaging.

"I have to protect my business. You are a threat to that. Hopefully now you realise that I am serious when I say that I intend to protect my interests."

"I never doubted that, Mr Callagher, but what I would like you to understand is that I have no interest in your business. My only interest has been to solve a murder. I am now confident that, while you are a criminal, you had nothing to do with the murder, so, in the absence of your other actions, we would have nothing left to say to each other."

Jim was offended at being characterised as a criminal. Some of his activities were not legal, of course, but he was a businessman. He traded in goods and provided services, and he was very successful at it. But there was something more here; an investigator who was not trying to catch him.

Saric continued. "I have to ask myself what to do about this situation. I asked you to leave my friend alone and you invaded his home and stole from him. You then threatened him. Ordinarily I would have to respond to this."

"Ordinarily?"

"Yes, you see, during the course of my work, I have found out enough about your business activities to put you in prison for a long time. The profits of the car business are far too high for the size of it, and we have evidence that it is a front to launder the money from your other interests."

"The police won't do anything; half of them are on my payroll. And if you do, it won't be the kid's toy next time."

"Maybe the police won't do anything, but maybe they will. Don't forget that I have friends too."

A pause. Jim thought for a moment. How sure was he that his contacts could protect him? Ten years ago, things were simple. His police contacts were easily bought with cash or drugs or girls, but things were changing. The people in charge were from a different generation and were not so easily bought. It would not take much for his people to lose control of the situation.

"The way I see it, you have a choice, Jim. You can take your chances with the police. Maybe it comes good, maybe it doesn't, but either way you will have me as an enemy, and believe me, that won't come good for you. Or you can take the other option."

Jim focused hard on not looking too interested. There was a deal to be done here, he could sense it. "What's that, then?"

"We go our separate ways. You promise me that you will never again threaten any of my friends, and I will make sure that the police don't look at anything other than the items they need to convict the killer.

"It's all about focus. If I tell them who did it and why, and feed them the details they need, then they'll be happy with that, get their conviction and move on. Nothing comes back to you.

"But what if instead of that I just tell them who did it and that it was connected with the accounting. Then there are forensic accountants pouring all over Tony Spencer's books for months. It'll be the end of you."

It hurt Jim to admit that the man sitting at his dining table scared him, but it was true. This man was dangerous, and despite wanting to take him on, he knew that was the wrong choice. Jim was a proud man, but he was not stupid.

"OK, Saric, I'll leave things, if you keep the police away from me."

As Saric left the large house and walked back up the long drive towards his car, which was parked a short distance down the road, he was pleased to have solved another problem, but he was also wondering how he was going to explain to Rob that he had to drop his anger against the man who had threatened the memory of his lost family.

CHAPTER 42

As Rob moved towards Saric's front door to let Phillip in, he wondered what Saric had thought of him the first time they met. It was easy to judge the responses of grieving spouses as correct or incorrect, based largely on some fictional idea of what grief or anger or loss should look like. Things were never this simple, there was no right way to grieve.

If Rob had thought Phillip to be arrogant or heartless when he had opened the door to him at their first meeting, he thought nothing of the sort now. The smart suit and expensive leather shoes had been replaced by worn jeans and a pair of trainers. His face was drawn, and his eyes tired.

There would be good days and bad days ahead for Phillip. For a moment, Rob envied how that process would be for him. At least he had certainty. There were answers, and even though they were painful, he would be able to bury his wife, mourn for her and visit her grave. For Rob, there were no answers and no certainties. He did not know whether his wife and son were dead or alive.

"Hi Phillip, thank you for coming."

"Do you have news?"

"Yes, please come in."

Rob showed Phillip to Saric's office. The same three coloured chairs were laid out, but there was no test this time, they were just chairs.

Over the next forty minutes, Saric and Rob talked Phillip through the case, the work they had performed and how his wife had been murdered by a lonely man who was desperate to protect the woman he loved. This softened the story slightly, and there would be time to fill in the gaps later, as the criminal case proceeded. For now, it was enough for Phillip to know that his wife's murderer had been found and that they had done enough work to be sure they had the right man.

As he showed Phillip out, Rob felt the same sense of responsibility that he felt every time they solved a case; that he should be able to do more. Solving the case was not enough; there were lives to be rebuilt. He knew that for Phillip, the pain was only just beginning, and he was sorry to have to leave him to do that alone.

"Do you think she knew?" Rob asked, as he placed a mug of coffee on Saric's desk.

"Who?" Saric was deep in concentration at his monitor.

"Sarah. She submitted the claims and received the money, so she must have seen that the numbers didn't add up. Do you think she knew what he was up to? When we suggested that she could have committed the fraud, were we really only using that to get him to confess?"

Saric took a long sip of coffee. "I don't know," was his honest reply. "I'm never surprised what people will do for the ones they love. But we weren't asked to investigate the fraud, only the murder. If Colin chooses to confess to the fraud too, then that's his choice."

Rob wanted to argue. He wanted to discuss whether a person's motive when committing a crime could affect whether the act was more or less immoral. He wanted to discuss whether covering up another person's crime out of love was acceptable, and he wanted to discuss whether they had a moral responsibility to tell the police about their suspicions.

He wanted to do all of those things, but only one thing really mattered now. Saric was staring at him.

"Rob, we need to talk about Helen."

Rob's chest tightened. He wanted to speak but anything he said would delay Saric telling him what he had found. He should stay calm, should accept that it was probably nothing, but even so his pulse was racing. He managed a slight nod.

"I've spoken to the lawyer who dealt with the will. He's retired now and very frail, but he says there are things we need to know. He is about to go in for a small operation and if everything goes alright he should be able to meet us in four weeks."